P9-EEG-506

# FALLING

# FALLING

*Harris Dulany*

*The McCall Publishing Company*

NEW YORK

*For Barry*



*Published simultaneously in Canada by*
*Doubleday Canada Ltd., Toronto*

*Library of Congress Catalog Card Number: 75-139529*

*SBN 8415-0087-8*

*The McCall Publishing Company*
*230 Park Avenue, New York, N.Y. 10017*

PRINTED IN THE UNITED STATES OF AMERICA

*Design by Tere LoPrete*

# FALLING

# I

Ronnie Mandeville dreams of falling. Endless terror. His eyelids twitch. His hands grip the sides of the cold bed. His legs thrash. His scream is muted by the paralysis of sleep, starting like an urgent sigh and ending in a moan. Down and down. The end is near. The barn floor. Water? Land? His body convulses on the wrinkled sheets as he tries to draw himself up. Falling quickly to the end, he awakens.

The bedroom is dark. The alarm has not sounded, but the clock ticks loudly in the heatless room. There are no rugs on the wide unpainted boards of the floor. Ronnie has been restless throughout the night, but now he huddles quietly under the warm quilts and blankets, waiting for the alarm clock to ring. His eyes are open, and he is watching snow fall through the branches of a maple tree outside his window. The branches and snow are illuminated by light from the kitchen below. He can hear water running from a faucet in the kitchen, a plate clinking against another plate, a refrigerator door thudding shut, a drawer full of utensils opening and closing. He looks at the clock as it begins to ring. A dog rushes into the room, wagging its tail. It licks his face. He does not move. The dog goes away. The alarm winds down and stops.

Ronnie Mandeville lies under the quilts and blankets planning the quickest route through the cold room and down the steep back stairs of the house. By mistake he has laid out his gas station uniform the night before. But today is the funeral and he will not have to put the uniform's clammy petroleum smell against his skin. He will never wear it again. He will need instead a sweater from the dresser, shirt and pants from the closet. Long underwear and socks are on the chair with the uniform. Boots are downstairs on newspaper in the rear hallway. In the dim light he can see his breath. He moves quickly around the room, filling his arms with clothes. At the stairs the dog blocks his path. He kicks at it with his bare foot.

The warm air of the kitchen envelops Ronnie. The step from the frozen boards in the hallway to the heated linoleum in the kitchen slows him, relaxes his tense rushing body. He moves to the kerosene range and dumps his clothing on the warm side of the black cast-iron surface. He grunts to his mother who is cooking oatmeal on the hot side of the green enamel range. Opening the oven door, he squats with his back to the warmth.

"I've told you not to come into the kitchen half-naked," she says. He is wearing the underwear he slept in.

He stands and spreads the clothing flat on the stove, then squats again and puts his hands inside the open oven.

"Build a fire in the living room when you get a chance," his mother tells him. He dresses except for his socks, and is no longer shivering.

"Who's the oatmeal for?" he asks.

The slight, thin-featured woman, whose abundant tied-back hair is the same brown color as his, does not answer.

"Save it for Bunnie when she gets up," he tells her.

"You'll need it, too," she snaps back. "It's cold and you'll be outside at the cemetery."

"It's cold and I'm outside every day."

In the bathroom he brushes his teeth and urinates and stands for a minute before the glowing coils of the electric wall heater.

When he returns to the kitchen, the oatmeal is ready, along with three fried eggs and two slices of buttered toast. He puts on his socks and eats.

In the hallway, Ronnie kneels on newspaper to tie his boots. He is wearing a red quilted jacket and a second pair of green and gray hunting socks into which his pants cuffs are tucked.

"What about the fire in the living room?" his mother shouts from the stove in the kitchen at the other end of the hall.

"I forgot," he says, untying the boots.

There is a dank odor in the cold living room. It comes from the body in the casket. The flowers in the room are three days old. There are not enough of them. Ronnie pulls the light chain and shadows dance around the room as the naked bulb swings in a narrow arc. The flowers, the coffin and himself sway and bounce on the faded cream and gold wallpaper designs. Crouching in his stockinged feet, Ronnie jams newspaper, sticks and logs into the stove, lights the paper with a match from the mantel above the chimney pipe hole, and shuts the door. While he is waiting for the logs to catch, he looks at his father in the casket. The undertaker has shaved Hank's sideburns and shortened his black crewcut. Virginia Jane requested that. His father looks young. He is only forty. The paper in the stove begins to roar. Ronnie partially shuts the chimney draft and waits for the logs to catch.

Hank is in the barn bent over the fender of one of his stock cars so that his torso is almost entirely inside the pink car. Ronnie's car roars into the driveway, skidding sideways on the frozen gravel. A massive eight-cylinder engine is suspended above Hank from a block and tackle attached to the barn's central beam. Ronnie powers the car out of its spin and slides to a stop near the doors. Even when Ronnie is standing beside him, the short sinewy man does not come up to greet him.

"I got a fight," Ronnie says.

A grunt comes from inside the guts of the car. It is an old car, a two-seater of the kind once called a coupé.

"Semi-final. How about that?"

"How did you do that?"

"I substitute this Thursday. Fight a kid from New Jersey. Pretty boy. Doesn't like to get hit in the face."

"Will you be ready in three days?" Hank asks.

Ronnie answers by dancing around the front of the car, jabbing and hooking fiercely at an invisible opponent. When he stops, he grins—and because one of his upper teeth is missing, he shuts his mouth quickly and rubs the back of his hand over his lips. The car has a white number 37 painted on each side. The paint of the 7 on the passenger side has run.

"Is he white?" Hank asks.

"Yeah. Good, too. He's fought in a couple of finals." Ronnie smooths his brown hair back from his forehead.

"Get me a ticket," Hank says from inside the car.

"I get two for free anyway. Do you really want to come?" Ronnie is openly pleased.

"Sure. I want to see you get your ass kicked."

Ronnie kicks at Hank's backside. Hank struggles out from under the engine block and collars his son. Laughing, they whoop and roll on the floor in mock violence.

In the living room the fire roars louder as the logs begin to catch.

The trophies are gone from the mantel and the shelves.

"Where are the trophies?" Ronnie shouts. "Where are all Hank's trophies?"

Virginia Jane comes into the living room drying the oatmeal bowl. "I put them in the barn," she says.

"Why?" Ronnie shouts.

"They were your father's."

"I'm still fighting tonight," Ronnie says suddenly.

"You told me you called it off," Virginia Jane says to him with surprise.

"But I didn't."

"You promised me you would."

"They couldn't get another substitute."

"It's not too late. Call them now."

Ronnie shakes his head and runs past her into the vestibule where he puts on his boots and leaves the house. The laces flap as he wades through the new snow and darkness to his car.

The drive to town from the Mandeville farm is not a long one. The funeral procession will come this way later. There are farms along this road and a dark section of spruce forest where shaded snow lasts well into May.

Ronnie knows the drive well, but it is still dark, and he sees only the road lined with banks of plowed snow and the soft flakes falling. He sees also the mailboxes dug clear and recessed in the shoulder-high banks. Occasionally his headlights catch a house on a turn. Here and there a kitchen light is on, a square of yellow beyond the darkness.

Ronnie has turned on the heater but the car is cold. The windshield wipers flap, but little of the dry snow sticks even beyond the circles. The tires turn softly over the hard-packed layer of snow on the road.

Ronnie snaps on the car radio, and when the sound warms on, he works the dial back and forth across the empty static, pausing at a farm report and then flipping across more static to a Boston station that wavers in and out with rude music that disrupts the stillness. He snaps the music off.

Halfway to town, he passes a plow, moving ponderously and spewing snow up on the right bank of the road. The car is harder to handle on the unpacked snow, but there is no danger since both sides of the road are cushioned by the high banks. The car enters the section of spruce forest, where some of the boughs of the trees are weighted with snow and hang down into the tunnel of his headlight world.

At twenty-one, Ronnie has had eight professional fights, and four of these he has won. He has never been knocked out in the ring, nor has he punched anyone else unconscious there. A cut above his eyebrow was bleeding so badly in one fight that he was not allowed to continue after the third round. The scar from that cut now splits his eyebrow horizontally into two parts. That was a technical knockout, but he has never been unconscious, at least not in public. His father, whom he will help bury today, knocked him against the edge of an open car door two winters ago, putting him out for almost a minute, but no one else saw it and his mother still does not know. He is not really a trained boxer, but he does take money for brawling four two-minute rounds in early preliminaries before the main event on Thursday nights in Portland, Maine, a half-hour drive from the farm. This makes him a professional. The money is not enough to live on, and he earns money for himself, his car, his motorcycle and his board by working in a gas station in the small town to which he is now traveling through the silent snowfall.

As the car tops the crest of the final hill that slopes gently down into the town, Ronnie can see a pre-dawn line of gray at the horizon of the ocean. There are streetlights in the town and ruts of snow on the street. Already fishermen are drinking coffee in the restaurant across from the gas station. There is no sound for Ronnie but the noise of the car. And snow, falling.

The car's distorted and vain mufflers rumble and crackle as it pulls into the gas station lot. The car is old, a '49 Ford, well cared for, navy-blue. The gas station is on the edge of a river, next to a turnbridge, just above a harbor. There are steps leading from the lot down to a dock with a gas pump on it. There are a few fishing boats in the harbor and none at the slips below the backs of the stores in the little inlets and water alleys of the town. A thick shelf of ice lines the pilings and rip-rap along these passageways. Thinner ice covers the water. Snow covers the ice. The tide is going out and the river rushes violently through the narrow passageway under the bridge. The car pulls beyond the gas pumps, its headlights momentarily catching the man seated at a desk inside the station. Its mufflers snarl when it stops, backing off with a string of sharp cracks. Then there is no sound except the water rushing, boiling under the bridge.

When Ronnie slams the door of the gas station, the plate

glass windows shudder. The tiny sound of the bell on the door continues for a moment like an afterthought. At the desk Boyd looks up from the morning paper in surprise. "What are you doing here?" he asks, removing his rimless glasses. The station is dimly lit by a ceiling bulb. On the desk is a fluorescent lamp that washes Boyd in gray light. "You don't have to work today," he says. "I'm closing the station from nine-thirty to three. And I can finish up after the funeral. As far as I know, everything's all set at the house. I just talked to your mother over the phone. She called to say you were on your way into town."

"Did she say I was coming here?"

"She didn't know where you were going, except toward town. Anyway, the hearse'll be there at eleven. I just talked to Mr. Stevens. He was a little worried about this snowfall, but I think it'll let up about midmorning. I still got to call Reverend Sloan and then get out there and plow your driveway."

The clock above the doorway to the garage says six-thirty. Mounted on the wall beside this doorway is a pay telephone and on a chair beneath it is a telephone book. Ronnie pushes the book to the floor and sits in the chair, tilting it against the wall. He props his wet boots on Boyd's desk. "I wanted to talk to you," he says.

"Certainly, son," Boyd says. "What is it?"

"Don't call me son," Ronnie shouts. "I'm not your son yet." He lashes out a backhand that catches Boyd in the middle of the face. Two more quick punches to the big man's solar plexus double him over. A right cross topples him to the floor.

Ronnie takes his feet off Boyd's desk. "I wanted to talk to you," he says.

"Certainly, son," Boyd says. "What is it?"

"I think I'm leaving."

"Leaving? What do you mean? Home?"

"No. Quitting. Here. I won't be coming back to work anymore."

Boyd carefully folds the paper. He stands up, a head taller than Ronnie, eighty pounds heavier.

"Let's go get some coffee, son," he says, taking a light beige cowboy hat from a hook near the door and putting it on over his close-cropped blond hair. He holds the door for Ronnie as they step out into the gray, softly falling snow.

Above the cash register on the back wall of the station is an old and faded poster advertising a 1954 rodeo in Dubois, Wyoming. One of the four featured riders on the poster, wearing a beige hat, is Bold Sam Boyd.

As they cross the snow-covered lot, they can hear the drone of a heavy boat engine coming from the water below them. A teen-age boy, the harbormaster's son, is sitting in the ice-breaker trembling and holding his hands as close as he dares to the warm muffler and exhaust pipe of the awkward-looking boat. He waves to them and then places his hand back near the pipe that rises like a flagpole from the middle of the boat. They cross the street, Boyd picking his way through the snow ruts in his western boots. The restaurant has a crude painting of a lobster trap and buoy on its sign. Before they enter they hear the ice-breaker engine increase in pitch. By the time they finish their coffee and doughnuts, the boy will have warmed the engine and circled the harbor twice to break up the thin salt ice. The boat will be moored and quiet, and the boy will be on his way to school.

There are mostly fishermen at the counter in the restaurant. They are not going out today. They know that the snow will stop by midmorning, but by noon the wind will have come up enough to prompt small-craft warnings. Any traps in precarious locations were brought in yesterday. The price they would get for their lobsters is high, but they are not going out. They have come from their homes to sit with each other through the snowfall, and later through the windy sunshine. They have made no promises to their wives. Several of them will spend part of the morning mending traps in sheds at the edge of the harbor. Some will return home in midmorning to put on suits and take their wives to Hank's funeral.

Ronnie is embarrassed by the abrupt silence his presence causes in the restaurant. His cousin, Harry Fry, a boisterous twenty-five-year-old with a wind-red face, three children and his own lobster boat, comes over to greet him and ask him quietly if he can help at all today. When he returns to the men he was sitting with, Ronnie can hear him finish a tale of some sexual escapade with an Indian girl in the back country. He whispers, but the men laugh violently at the conclusion of the tale. The owner of the restaurant, comes out of the kitchen in his undershirt, takes the coffee from the waitress and brings it to Ronnie and Boyd.

"I'm awfully sorry about your dad," he says to Ronnie. He touches Ronnie's arm. His fingers are wet and clean, and his arm is covered with black hair that has drops of water and flecks of potato clinging to it.

Ronnie looks at the sugar he is spooning into the coffee and says: "Thanks."

When the man goes back to his kitchen, Boyd asks: "What will you do for work?"

Several of the fishermen look up from their coffee. The waitress stands nearby.

"I don't know," Ronnie says softly.

"Why don't you just take a couple of weeks off and then come back to work. It would do you good, and Del and me can handle the station."

Ronnie shakes his head no and sips his coffee.

Boyd lowers his voice and says: "Boy, I guess you know

something about my plans by now, and how they include your mother. Well, they include you, too. I want you to run that gas station for me once you're in the family."

Ronnie shakes his head no.

"That way I can spend more time at the ranch. Build that into something." He bends closer and lowers his voice even more, although it is not necessary because Harry Fry and the older men and even the waitress are laughing loudly about something. "Do you know I have an option on the Wilson place?" Boyd tells him and draws back to observe his reaction. Ronnie looks at him blankly, and Boyd says: "If I buy it, then my spread and your mother's farm are connected. We can run the biggest darn herd of cattle in New England."

Ronnie stares into his coffee.

"Beef is the coming thing in this state. They now know that potato pulp is a good feed for them. That's what the people at the agricultural station at U-Maine say, and they ought to know."

Ronnie looks away, looks at his watch, looks at the waitress, looks at the wall clock.

Boyd pauses to drink some coffee, and then says abruptly: "You're not thinking of leaving home, are you, boy?"

Ronnie shakes his head no.

Boyd offers to pay for the coffee, but Ronnie stands up from his stool and puts a dime by the half-empty cup.

"I'll talk to you later," Boyd says and stays behind in the restaurant.

Outside, the street is filling with snow that has not been plowed yet. Ronnie brushes his hair away from his eyes. In the early light, there is a pink and gray tint to the snow. The pick-up trucks belonging to the fishermen are parked along the curb with their motors running. Ronnie waits while a car with its headlights on rolls by in the rutted snow. The street seems enclosed and silent, even with the hum of the truck engines. A sudden wind drives snow into Ronnie's face, and he hurries to his car.

On the return trip, the road to the farm is cleared. It is hard to tell if the dawn is complete yet because of the overcast from the snowclouds. When Ronnie pulls into the yard the dog barks and runs beside the car. It wags its tail and jumps on Ronnie's leg as he walks to the house. He leans down to scratch the dog's head.

In the hallway, as he bends to remove his boots, Ronnie shouts to Virginia Jane but she does not answer his greetings. As he enters the kitchen he sees that she is bent over the sink, washing the good china that is kept wrapped in newspaper in boxes in the cold pantry behind the kitchen. There is a pile of crumpled newspapers at her feet, some of it multi-colored Sunday comics, and a cardboard box on the drainboard with more exploded newspaper inside it. Ronnie greets her again but Virginia Jane does not look up from the sink. He rushes at her and pushes her from the loft and she falls slowly to the floor far below. She strikes the front fender of the pink car and slides to the floor. He knows that Boyd has telephoned her. He asks her why she is washing dishes that are already clean, but she does not answer this either and continues to look down at her task in the sink. Ronnie turns and goes down the hall to the bathroom. He surprises his sixteen-year-old sister who is standing on a footstool stretching her neck so she can see her body in the medicine cabinet mirror. Her small breasts are naked and she wears white wool socks and plain cotton underpants. When she sees him, she covers each breast with a cupped hand and Ronnie goes back into the hall, shutting the door.

"Check the living-room fire," Virginia Jane tells him when he re-enters the kitchen.

"If you get that room too hot, he's going to smell," Ronnie tells her.

Her shoulders bunch up as she stands at the sink. The cup she is drying drops to the floor and bounces on the linoleum. She does not turn to face him as she slowly squats to pick it up.

In the living room it is light enough to work. Outside, the snow has stopped and the sky seems less overcast. The wind flaps the clear plastic that is taped outside the windows. Ronnie selects four heavy oak logs from the pile behind the stove. With a little shoving these fill the warm stove. Ronnie glances at Hank and turns the damper until the chimney is wide open. In a few moments the logs catch and the hard draft begins to make the fire roar.

Back in the kitchen, Ronnie sits at the cleared table. Virginia Jane turns to talk to him, but he cuts her off rudely by asking: "Is there any more coffee?"

She dutifully pours a cupful and sets it in front of him. She sits at the table and, looking directly at Ronnie, she asks:

"Are you leaving?"

"Did Boyd call you?" Ronnie counters.

"Are you leaving?" she insists.

"No," Ronnie lies, toying with the salt shaker.

"Mr. Boyd said you would."

"Who do you believe? Me or Boyd?" Ronnie bends to blow on his hot coffee.

"But you did quit."

"Yes, I quit."

"What will you do?" Now Virginia Jane looks down at the dishtowel in her lap, perhaps to allow him to continue to lie.

"I'll get another job."

"Doing what?"

"I don't know. Maybe at Farley's, delivering oil." Ronnie sprinkles some salt on the table and pushes it into a pile with his finger.

"Do they need someone at Farley's?"

"I don't know."

"Did you ask?"

"Not yet."

"What's wrong with Mr. Boyd's job?"

"What's wrong with Mr. Boyd?" Ronnie says, looking at her for the first time.

"What do you mean?"

"I don't want to be part of a merger."

"What do you mean?"

"With Boyd and the Wilson place."

"What are you talking about?"

"Do we own this farm, or does Grandpa Simmons?" Ronnie asks.

"Why?"

"Do we?" he insists.

"We have title to it."

"Does Boyd know that?"

"I don't see the point of this."

"Is Grandpa Simmons coming to the funeral?"

Virginia Jane stands up. "If he can," she says coldly and turns her back on him and walks to the sink.

Bunnie comes out of the bathroom then, as if she had been waiting for the argument to end. She is wearing a bra now, and as she passes through the kitchen without speaking, Ronnie stares at her thin body. She stares defiantly back at him, and he laughs out loud. "Next time lock the door," he says.

"What?" Virginia Jane asks and turns to face him.

"Nothing. I was talking to Bunnie." Ronnie has turned in his chair so he can watch Bunnie walk up the back stairs. When she is gone, he stands up and walks down the hall to the bathroom.

"Shovel the front steps before you go anywhere," Virginia Jane shouts after him.

"I'm only going to the bathroom," Ronnie says and locks the door. He is not sure she heard him. Standing on the stool Bunnie had used earlier, he masturbates, discharging his semen into a wad of toilet paper.

# II

There is no plastic outside the windows of Ronnie's room. The wind that is rapidly clearing the sky rattles the panes and blows across Ronnie's back as he stacks sweaters and shirts neatly into the suitcase spread open on the floor. The warmth from the lower part of the house—the hot living room is directly beneath him—is melting the ice patterns on the window. But Ronnie still shivers from the cold. Outside, the clouds begin to open, and white sunlight suddenly falls through the two southern windows. The wind beats against the panes more violently. Ronnie is startled to hear footsteps on the back stairs. He pushes the suitcase under his bed. The dog rushes into the room wagging its tail. Ronnie stands up quickly and begins to unbutton his shirt. Virginia Jane, wearing a shiny black dress and carrying a black hat and veil, follows the dog into the room. A white knit shawl is draped around her shoulders.

"What are you doing?" she asks.

"Dressing for the funeral," Ronnie answers without facing her.

She seems distracted. She seems not to have heard him. Ronnie removes his shirt. Virginia Jane sits on the edge of the bed, half-turned toward him. Ronnie unzips the fly of his pants and she turns her back to him and faces the open door. Downstairs in the rear of the house, Bunnie is using the bathroom and they can hear the toilet flush. Ronnie drops his pants and steps out of them. In his off-white long underwear, he walks to the closet to get the pants to his suit.

"Have you called yet?" Virginia Jane asks. She looks straight ahead through the door.

"Called who?" Ronnie asks.

"Your promoter." For emphasis she turns to look at him. He is standing bow-legged with his hands in his underwear adjusting his testicles. He stops abruptly, and she turns away. The invasion of his privacy angers him and suddenly he is shouting at her:

"Don't start that again. I am not calling it off. I can't. It's too late. It's an important fight. A semi-final. I won't do it. I will not blow the best chance I've ever had in my life. I get one hundred dollars. For no more than eighteen minutes work. That's what you want, for me to lose that chance. The funeral ends this morning. The fight is tonight. I don't see what they have to do with each other. There's no one to substitute. Gus wouldn't let me anyway. Hank was coming to this fight. The first one he ever came to. Why don't you use his ticket? *He* wanted me to fight."

He has the urge to hit her in the back of the head with his fist. He even anticipates the solid roundness of her skull and the sound his punch will make—a combination of a crack and a thud—and how much, if any, pain it will cause to his fist. Perhaps he will break a bone in his hand. Both his fists are clenched tightly and he raises them above his head and screams in a great explosion of breath:

"Yaaaaaaaaaaaaaa."

Several times a week six-year-old Ronnie goes from the town school where he attends first grade to the Chevrolet garage on High Street where his father works as a mechanic. To the child, Hank's work is magical. In a different way, the owner of the garage thinks so too, since Hank is one of the best mechanics in Maine. As a kid, he started with bicycles and farm machinery on his father's small farm in Iowa, and progressed to motorcycles and cars before he was a teen-ager, and then on to airplanes for the Navy during the war. Ronnie watches his father or plays in the garage or out in the warm showroom when the owner is not there.

Often when Hank is finished at five o'clock, he takes Ronnie around with him in the pick-up truck to bars in neighboring towns. While Hank drinks, Ronnie waits in the truck. If it is cold, as it is tonight, he comes inside with Hank and stands below him at the bar. The bars are called beer halls because they do not serve whiskey, and most of them have wood or coal stoves and sawdust on the floor. Some of them look like grocery stores to Ronnie, with canned goods stacked on shelves around the walls and racks for bread near the counter where the beer is served. The men in these bars are rough men:

loggers, farmers, fishermen, truck drivers, mechanics. They are friendly to Ronnie, but even when they play with him or give him candy, they frighten him. He enjoys being with his father, however, and he stays as close to him as possible and tries to hide from the men. If there is a woman in the bar, she makes a fuss over him, breathing her beer on him. The women annoy him, because the fuss they make seems to be for the benefit of the men in the bar, and because these women don't seem like any that he has ever known.

One of these women has him now. She has seated him up on the bar and is trying to kiss him on the cheek. In one hand Ronnie holds a half-eaten bean sandwich. Ketchup is dripping from the sandwich and Ronnie is trying to keep this away from his school pants and fend off the woman's kisses at the same time. It is cold in the bar, and he is wearing his heavy winter coat with the hood, which presses up around his chin as he struggles. He rotates his head furiously, but as he does this, their lips meet and catch, and through the bite of bean sandwich and ketchup, he can taste beer and lipstick. He is comfortable there being kissed, but he continues to struggle as he is expected to do. The woman stands back at arm's length and looks at him and says: "Boy, you sure don't take to affection." Everyone at the bar laughs except Hank, who pulls Ronnie away. The child takes another bite of his sandwich.

They are out later than ever before. This is the fifth bar they have visited in three towns. They seldom come to this one. Hank is buying whatever food or candy Ronnie asks for. It is dark and before supper. When they leave the bar, Ronnie notices the air has become cold enough to freeze his nostrils together when he breathes through them. The snow squeaks under his boots and is impossible to pack into snowballs. Hank has left the truck running, and it is warm inside the cab. Ronnie stands on the seat and they drive away from the town out into the country. Ronnie cannot remember ever being on this road before. Through the lighted windows they pass, he can see women preparing supper. He sees a family already seated at a kitchen table eating, and at another farm a small girl looking out an upstairs window, silhouetted by a light at her back. There is no moon yet and between the farms it is very dark except for the stars in the sky. They come to a crossroad with a filling station already closed for the night and a general store–post office that has a dim light in it. Hank stops in front of this building, but it is also closed and he knocks on the door. An old woman finally comes through the store from the back, wearing an apron and chewing a bite of her supper. Hank asks some directions that Ronnie does not hear, and when he gets back in the car, the boy asks if they are lost. The man does not reply, and the silence of the ride continues as they turn at the crossroad and drive out an unpaved road that quickly dissolves into one lane. They are in a forest, and the headlights show only pine trees with no breaks between them. When they come on more open land, there is a farm on the right at the end of a long driveway that has been plowed clear of snow. Hank turns in here and as they reach the end of the driveway, Ronnie sees a man in a blue denim coat walk under the yard light, carrying a bucket filled with eggs. A woman looks out from her kitchen. The man stops in the driveway and waits for Hank's truck to pull up next to him. Hank rolls his window down and when the man sees him, he says: "What can I do for you, son?" Ronnie can see a four- or five-day growth of whiskers on the man's face. "Does Carl Timmons live here?" Hank asks. "Next place on the right," the man says. Hank is already driving away, around the plowed circle in front of the house, as the man shouts: "It's just a cabin. You can miss it if there ain't no lights on." As they pass the house, Ronnie looks at the woman still peering from her kitchen window.

Farther down the road there is a light on in the cabin, and Ronnie catches a glimpse of a man walking by in the back of the room. There is a short driveway, but it is not plowed, and Hank parks the truck on the road, jamming it against the bank of snow so cars can pass, although it is doubtful that there will be any cars on this dark woods road. He leaves the motor running and the parking lights on, but when Ronnie starts to get out on his side, he tells him to stay put. Hank takes off his gloves and leaves them in the car. There is a small roofed porch on the front of the cabin and a path beaten down in the snow leading up to this. Hank goes to the foot of the porch steps and stops and calls the man's name. Ronnie can see Carl Timmons cross his view through the kitchen window on his way to the front door. Wood smoke curls up from the chimney pipe on the roof. Hank calls again and the porch light goes on. Carl Timmons comes out on the porch wearing suspenders over the top of his long underwear. "Who's that?" he asks. Hank says his name, and Timmons asks, "What can I do for you?" as he comes down the steps. Hank does not reply. As Timmons steps off the last step and before his foot touches the ground, Hank hits him in the middle of the face with his fist. Timmons sprawls up the steps and lands on his back on the porch. Hank does not wait for him to get up; instead he takes the steps at one leap and dives on the man, hitting him quickly and with force several times again in the face before the man throws him aside and stumbles down off the porch into the snow. Ronnie cannot see the man's face but he assumes he is bleeding because he holds the back of his hand to his mouth. Hank races down the steps after the man and spins him around and swings at him again, but the man blocks the punch and throws one of his own. Now that they are level with each other, Ronnie can see that Timmons is tall, and Hank must punch up at him. There is another exchange of punches and Hank topples backwards into the deep snow. Timmons does not follow him, but stands on the path and waits for him to get up. Timmons is breathing hard and now Ronnie can see that his nose is bleeding. He wipes at it with the sleeve of his underwear. Hank gets up cautiously and when Timmons swings a punch at him, Hank is able to duck under it and hit the man in the stomach. Timmons doubles over and Hank, with his heavy work boots, kicks up into the man's descending face. Timmons flies back against the porch railing, snapping it in half, and as he lies there bent backwards over the edge of the porch, Hank stands watching him, trying to catch his breath. Timmons rolls his head from side to side and then sits up abruptly and spits a mouthful of blood into the snow. He hangs his head down and his hands fall between his knees. Hank continues to watch while he brushes snow from his clothes. When Hank's clothes are cleared of snow and he is breathing less heavily, he seems satisfied and turns to walk back to the truck. He is about halfway to the truck when Timmons takes part of the broken two-by-four that served as a porch railing, wrenches it free from its corner post and races after Hank with it. Ronnie's window is open and he shouts: "Dad!" Hank turns around but has time only to run into the snow. Trying to turn quickly to chase him, Timmons falls. Hank is back on him before he can get up, and then it is Hank who has the two-by-four. Timmons is halfway to his feet and Hank swings the board like a baseball bat and catches Timmons on the side of the head. Ronnie can see blood gush from the man's hair. Timmons goes down to one knee and his hands drop limply to his sides. Nearly unconscious, he raises his face to look at Hank, and Hank strikes downward with the board, breaking it in half over Timmons' upturned forehead. The man crumples into the snow. Hank drops the board and stands over him, his chest heaving. Ronnie can see blood spilling from Timmons' face and head and spreading through the snow. Involuntarily he begins to cry, and to keep Hank from hearing him, he rolls up the window. Hank stumbles to the steps of the porch and sits on them while he catches his breath. He puts his head in his hands and stays that way for a long time, long enough for the boy to control his crying.

When Hank returns to the car, he must walk in the deep snow to circle the crumpled heap of Timmons on the beaten path. He does not look at the heap. Hank's right eye is swollen shut, and since this is the only eye Ronnie sees on the ride home, he wonders how his father can drive. Hank drives with one hand and keeps the other, the broken one, cradled in his lap.

The thin end of the tie comes out longer than the fat end, and Ronnie must undo the knot and start again. He hears Boyd's jeep plowing the snow of the driveway. The wind is blowing the maple tree branches wildly outside the window. Ronnie reaches the window just as Boyd gets out of the jeep and hurries out of sight under the porch roof holding down his cowboy hat. But as Ronnie turns from the window, he doesn't hear Boyd come through the front door. He looks over his shoulder in time to see Boyd returning to his jeep. He thinks for a moment that Boyd is leaving, and then he sees the black hearse moving slowly up the driveway. Boyd ducks back into the jeep and moves it so the hearse can park near the porch. Ronnie walks back to the mirror and struggles with his tie for a moment; and then, leaving it untied and dangling from his buttoned collar, he hurries down the back stairs in his stockinged feet. He is out on the porch standing beside Boyd by the time the boy gets out of the hearse.

The boy is Timothy Stevens, the undertaker's son, dressed in a shiny black suit. His pants are too short and the edges of his long underwear can be seen where they meet his white socks. Even though his collar is several finger widths too large, it looks uncomfortable. He wears black dress shoes and has difficulty negotiating the lumpy snow. He comes around the hearse, bracing himself against the hood and holding his glasses. Boyd offers him a hand to help him up the treacherous steps.

"Where's your dad?" Boyd shouts against the wind.

"Preacher's funeral in Holt's Mills," the boy answers.

"He told me this morning that he was driving," Boyd says, holding his hat.

"I don't believe so," Timothy answers.

Ronnie's feet are cold, so he turns and goes inside. Boyd and Timothy follow him. Virginia Jane meets them at the door and the four of them stand in the hallway while Boyd takes his jacket off and pulls off his western boots.

Finally it is Ronnie who blurts out: "What are you doing here?"

"Driving," Timothy answers simply.

"But it's not for an hour yet," Ronnie tells him, and the boy, who is two years younger than Ronnie, looks at him incredulously.

"I thought it was at ten o'clock," Timothy says to Virginia Jane.

"Eleven," she tells him. Ronnie turns from the group and bounds up the stairs to his room.

As Ronnie wrestles with his tie, he hears Virginia Jane fixing coffee for the young undertaker. The tie comes out right this time. Ronnie lets the knot hang loose. He puts on the coat to the blue suit and before he goes downstairs, he checks his suitcase. Satisfied that he has packed everything, he snaps it shut and pushes it back beneath the bed. As he turns to leave, he sees his sister standing in the doorway, watching him.

"You don't make much noise," he says to her.

"Going somewhere?" she asks.

She too is dressing for the funeral and is wearing a short suède skirt and gold sweater. She wears stockings but she is shoeless. In these clothes she looks much younger than she did standing on the bathroom stool. She repeats:

"Where are you going with the suitcase?"

"Away," he answers.

"Where?"

"None of your business, and you better not tell her until I'm gone."

He starts to walk out of the room, but she touches his arm and says: "Are you taking your car?"

"Yes," he says and stops in the doorway where he is close enough to smell the soap she washed with.

"Take me with you," she whispers, squeezing his arm.

"No." He pulls his arm away.

"Please," she says. He does not answer her again, but turns away and goes down the stairs. Halfway down he turns to look up at her, and when he puts his index finger to his lips to ask her silence, she shakes her head in agreement and goes down the hall to her room.

In the kitchen Ronnie finds Timothy Stevens sitting alone sipping coffee. When he asks him where Virginia Jane is, the boy points in the direction of the bathroom. Ronnie is standing in the middle of the kitchen floor waiting for her to come out when the telephone rings.

The phone is mounted on the wall by the window and Ronnie takes one step and picks it up before it rings a second time.

An old man on the other end of the line asks for "Ginny," and Ronnie covers the mouthpiece and shouts: "Mother. It's Grandpa Simmons." Ronnie can hear the toilet flush, and a moment later Virginia Jane rushes down the hall, trailed by the sound of gurgling water.

Ronnie stands beside her, looking absently through the window while she talks. Boyd walks from the barn with an ax and a bucketful of rock salt for the ice on the porch steps. This surprises him because he was somehow aware of Boyd's presence in the house.

Virginia Jane places the receiver back on its hook. She seems surprised and a little dazed, but she says: "That was your grandfather. He came all the way from St. Petersburg by bus. He's at the restaurant and he wants someone to pick him up."

"Why don't you and Boyd go?" Ronnie says. "I'll finish clearing those steps while you're gone. Take my car."

Virginia Jane takes the keys that Ronnie offers and goes to the back hallway where she exchanges her bedroom slippers for rubber snow boots. She puts a blue quilted ski parka on over her slight shoulders and goes outside. Boyd, still hanging onto his hat, has just put the bucket down. He looks up at her. Ronnie cannot hear what she tells him, but they go to the Ford, and with Boyd driving they turn out of the driveway, heading for town.

Ronnie moves from the window and looks at Timothy Stevens who holds up his empty coffee cup and asks: "Can I have some more coffee, Ron?"

"Sure. It's on the stove," Ronnie says. Without offering to get it for him, Ronnie goes out into the hall where he slips on his boots. Without tying them or putting his jacket on, he goes outside, bypassing the ax and the bucket of salt, headed for the barn.

The morning's fresh snow has covered the wooden ramp leading up to the open door of the barn. The edge of the space cleared by Boyd's jeep plow is piled knee-high with chunks of the new snow. It is the first time Ronnie can remember that the drive ramp into the barn has not been cleared after a storm. He must wade through this snow to get into the barn, and as he does, the snow tumbles into his unlaced boots each time he puts his foot down. Ronnie stands just inside the door until his eyes adjust to the dark. With the snow melting in his boots and the wind blowing through his white shirt, he begins to shiver. Although it is very cold, he can detect the faint smell of gasoline and grain. He can see the pink coupé, numbered 37, sitting in the middle of the barn floor, and the ropes dangling down into its open engine space. Tiny pieces of light shine through spaces between the boards in the roof. Ronnie sees the section of floor that has been scrubbed clean around and beyond the right fender of the car, a circle perhaps ten feet in diameter. Ronnie approaches this circle and drops to one knee. There is still a slight stain from the puddle of blood and urine that drained from his father's broken body. He stands and scans the edges and corners of the barn, looking for his father's trophies. Virginia Jane may have thrown them out and told him they were in the barn just to appease him. Ronnie is therefore surprised to see them all neatly set out on the shelf above Hank's workbench, all forty of them, plated with gold or silver, some with little cars at their pinnacles. The largest trophies and the four silver bowls are in the center, and the smallest are at the outer edges. Nailed to the wall behind the trophies is the multi-colored collection of license plates started by Virginia Jane's father in 1928 and continued by Hank.

Ronnie hurries to the trophies and, leaning over the bench, gathers the four silver bowls awkwardly in his arms. Each of the bowls has the same lettering, being prizes for the top driver of the summer at the Portland Speedway. Three of them—1958, 1962 and 1963—have Hank Mandeville engraved on them, and 1954 is inscribed to Henry Mandeville, since Hank was not too well-known in the state then, having only returned to his wife and son and infant daughter a little over a year before. The dates on the trophies do not go beyond the summer of 1964, the year of Hank's crippling motorcycle accident.

Ronnie tromps through the snow at the edge of the driveway with his load and as he is about to step out onto the cleared area, he slips and sits down in the bank. Cold snow falls into the back of his pants. Without putting any of the bowls down, he sits forward into a crouch and stands up. On the porch, he presses his load against the door and manages to turn the knob. Timothy Stevens looks up from his coffee as Ronnie passes through the kitchen. "Can I help?" the boy asks. "No," Ronnie answers.

The warm living room is bright with sunlight falling through the two southern windows and their plastic outer coating. There is a scent of pine in the room. After Ronnie has placed the four bowls carefully on the carpet in front of the cool stove, he takes one of the folding chairs from the row nearest the casket, stands on it and finds the pine air-freshener spray that Virginia Jane has hidden on the top shelf behind the stove. He puts the can down on the carpet, and removes the vases of flowers she has placed on the shelves. Then he lifts the silver bowls back into their original places. On the way out he picks up the spray can, and when he gets to the barn he tosses it in one of the garbage cans standing against the inside wall.

It takes him six trips to get the trophies back in place

on the shelves and mantel. He falls once on the treacherous porch steps, tearing his shirt and causing one of the smaller trophies to come loose from its black plastic base. Timothy Stevens asks him three times if he can help him. On the third trip Ronnie tells him to stop asking, but Timothy continues to look up anxiously each time Ronnie passes through the kitchen with an armload of trophies.

The last trophy he puts up is a gold one given to Hank for winning first place in the Fourth of July feature race at West Liberty, Iowa, in 1948. Ronnie was three years old when Hank won the trophy. The family was living then on Hank's father's farm near Columbus Junction, Iowa. Hank had returned there after the war and sent for his wife and infant son, who were here on this Maine farm with Virginia Jane's parents. Hank met Virginia Jane at a USO dance at the base in Pensacola, Florida, where she was a hostess. They married hastily when she became pregnant with Ronnie, and it was not until she had joined him in Iowa in 1947—against her parents' wishes—that Hank had ever seen his infant son. They went to work to help Hank's father save his small farm, but Hank preferred machinery to soybeans and corn. He was about to give it up and go to work as a mechanic when the old man died and left the farm to his brother, who sold it out from underneath them. They came to Maine in 1949 to live for two years in a second-floor apartment in town near the spot where Boyd now has his gas station.

Neither Hank, with his swollen eye and broken hand, nor Ronnie, standing on the seat holding his hands in his mouth to stifle his spasms of crying, speak on the drive home. Ronnie is hungry and tired, and his eyes hurt as he forces himself to look out through the window into the cold dark night. Grandma Simmons is at the apartment when they return, and she feeds Ronnie and puts him to bed. His father has murdered a man. His mother and Grandpa Simmons are out somewhere in the cold night. From his bedroom window Ronnie watches his father put a small suitcase into the cab of the truck–setting it down first in the snow so he can open the door with his good hand.

Hank drives away under the streetlight next to the bridge.

Two years later Hank returns, barreling on a motorcycle up the driveway of the Simmons farm where Virginia Jane, eight-year-old Ronnie and infant Bunnie live with Virginia Jane's parents. He tosses his dusty bedroll on the porch. Showered, shaved, he eats supper with the family, whose silence is testy rather than surprised. Evidently he was expected, although Ronnie is surprised. The next day he goes back to work at the Chevrolet garage in town. Bunnie was too young to care about Hank then. But by then Ronnie knows that her real father lies in a heap in front of a cabin somewhere in the next county.

This then is Ronnie's secret. That Carl Timmons is Bunnie's father. Virginia Jane knows this, but she does not know that Ronnie knows. Grandma Simmons carried it with her to the grave six months after Hank returned. That same winter Grandpa Simmons carried it to a house trailer in St. Petersburg, Florida, where he fled, leaving the farm in Hank's care.

There was another secret. That Hank murdered Carl Timmons. This secret Ronnie kept until he was fourteen. Hank had given him a motorcycle to ride on back roads around the farm, until he was old enough for a license. One summer day Ronnie drove every road he could find, searching for Carl Timmons' cabin. Ronnie found it, looking almost the same except for the growth of trees and weeds around it instead of snow. Inside he found a rock-faced couple in their seventies who told him that their son, Carl, had gone to California where he was now a guard in an amusement park near San Francisco. Ronnie did not identify himself, nor did he tell anyone about his visit to the cabin. Not even Hank, who smashed the spark plug of the motorcycle with a hammer because Ronnie had taken it beyond the limits set for him. Where and when had Hank found out that Carl Timmons was alive? Had they met in the amusement park? Did Hank and Virginia Jane correspond? Everyone but Ronnie knew Hank was coming back the day he arrived. And love-child Bunnie who never knew what happened in the snow after dark and before supper at that cabin. Or that her real father was an amusement park watchman at the other end of the country, instead of lying stiff with his side-burns cut off in the hot living room.

Until the day he jerked the rope out of Hank's hands in the top loft of the barn, Ronnie had never crossed his father. Not even one day two years before when Hank punched him six times on the run across the yard until Ronnie had back-pedaled into the edge of an open door on one of Hank's stock cars and knocked himself silly. Only Ronnie knew what Hank was capable of, and that he was about to do to Sam Boyd what he had done to Carl Timmons—and perhaps for the same reasons—if he had not been killed himself.

The day is still very cold. The sun, riding the clear southern sky, beams the blank midmorning light on the crowd of people shivering in the wind-blown yard. The people squint against the glare from the new snow and the clean white of the house. As they wait, they stamp their feet against the cold. A bed of insulating pine boughs lines the base of the house. This is half buried in accumulated and plowed snow, as is the bottom step to the front porch, which has been trampled to a lumpy slickness. The ax and bucket of rock salt still sit beside the step. The six men bearing the pall (led by Boyd and Ronnie) curse the unshoveled steps and huff their white-tongued breath at each other. The coffin slants on the descent, shifting the weight to Ronnie and Boyd on the front end. The people in the yard, murmuring politely and edging to their cars, pause to watch this precarious feat. The men touch their feet down with hesitation, feeling at the irregular ice on the steps. The crowd holds its frosty breath. Someone has slipped, and the men are struggling to make it right. The scene suspends. Too long. The men strain, motionless. And then abandon and sprawl to left and right as the coffin bounces on its corner and settles upside down beneath a bare bush near the steps. The crowd gasps. One expects applause. The men slap snow from their coats and pants, retrieve the errant box, help it into the waiting hearse. A corner of the coffin is dented. The cold people hurry to their cars.

Boyd returns to the steps and scatters rock salt on them. Sobbing can be heard inside the house. Ronnie shuts the rear door of the hearse and goes to his car to sit like the others, with motors running, waiting. Virginia Jane leaves the house now with a black veil over her face. Bunnie, the crier, steps out behind her, twitching with spasms of grief and holding a handkerchief to her eyes. She is followed by Grandpa Simmons, whose tiny leathered face is a deep bronze from the Florida sun. All three of them stand together at the edge of the steps, all with the same thin features, and all three the same height. Grandpa Simmons wears a long, black overcoat that is unbuttoned and reveals his gray suit, white shirt and tie, as well as his shaky bowed legs. His tanned hands are without gloves and he supports himself with a cane. Virginia Jane is almost obscured. Her black overcoat reaches below her knees, and she wears plain stockings and black shoes. Bunnie is hatless and her blond hair falls over the front of her shoulders to just above the slight rise in her gold sweater where her breasts are. She wears a chocolate suède blazer unbuttoned at the front and without lapels. The matching skirt stops well above her knees. She looks up from her handkerchief and her eyes are inflamed from crying. The three of them stand together until Boyd finishes sprinkling the salt. He offers his hand to Virginia Jane and helps her down the steps, and then helps Grandpa Simmons in the same way. Bunnie comes down the steps without his assistance. "I told him to shovel these steps," Virginia Jane says as she takes Boyd's arm. Bunnie starts to walk away from the group, and Virginia Jane says, "Come along, Bernice. We'll go in Mr. Boyd's station wagon with Grandpa Simmons and Reverend Sloan."

"I'll go with Ronnie," the girl answers without turning. "He can't go alone."

Virginia Jane holds Boyd's arm as they walk toward his blue station wagon. They are trailed by suntanned Grandpa Simmons and, farther back, the minister in his black overcoat. A sudden gust of wind almost knocks the tiny old man over, and Reverend Sloan hurries up to him and takes his arm.

Hank takes Grandpa Simmons' arm. They are standing on Route One waiting for the Boston bus. Grandpa Simmons wears a suit and a bowtie. Next to him is the suitcase he is taking with him to Florida. Hank's car idles beside the road, the wisps of vapor from its exhaust pipe blowing away each time a car speeds by. It is late winter and there is a crusted snow cover on the ground, but the day is sunny and still.

"Don't stay too long," Hank tells the old man.

Grandpa Simmons does not answer, just pulls his arm out of Hank's grip. Little Ronnie watches the two men nervously. Virginia Jane is not here to stop their arguments. She had to stay home with infant Bunnie who is running a fever. Hank has come out from the Chevy garage in his greasy mechanic's overalls to drive the old man to the bus stop.

Ronnie watches the horizon for the bus. He wonders why these two men fight; why Grandpa Simmons does not like Hank. He knows it has something to do with his mother. But what?

"I'm sorry," Hank says, offering the remark half-heartedly. "I hope when you come back, you'll see things differently."

"If things work out, I may not be back," Grandpa Simmons says, staring at the road, not looking at Hank or Ronnie.

"There's always a place for you," Hank says.

"Hopefully, yes," Grandpa Simmons says. "It *is* my property."

The bus appears. Ronnie wonders if Grandpa Simmons will continue to ignore him because he is angry with Hank.

The bus stops and its engine growls in idle. Ronnie smells the diesel smoke and feels its warmth. The door whooshes open and Ronnie sees the driver looking down at them curiously from the dark interior. He is wearing sunglasses and a gray shirt with the sleeves rolled up.

Grandpa Simmons bends and shakes Ronnie's hand. "Take care of your mother, Ronald," he says, and bends farther to pick up his suitcase.

Again Hank takes his arm, and again the old man shakes him off. Northbound traffic has prevented southbound cars from passing the bus, and a line begins to pile up behind the bus. Grandpa Simmons steps up into the darkness, and the driver, looking anxiously into his side mirror, pulls the door shut behind him.

Ronnie holds his breath against the blast of diesel smoke as the bus pulls out.

"Do you want to go to the garage with me for the rest of the afternoon?" Hank asks.

"Yes," Ronnie says, but he continues to watch the procession of bus and cars until it passes over the next hill and is gone.

The town police car leads the funeral procession. The blue light on the roof of the black car revolves slowly. Behind the police car is the hearse, driven by Timothy Stevens who is smoking a cigarette and fingering the pimples on the back of his neck. Boyd's blue station wagon follows next. In the front seat, Boyd in his light tan cowboy hat and Virginia Jane, her black veil obscuring her face, stare straight ahead. Grandpa Simmons, in the back seat, maintains a grim silence, his short jaw set tightly shut, his eyes on Boyd's hat, his hands folded over his smooth black cane. He nods occasionally to Reverend Sloan who, seated beside him, tries to talk with the three silent figures. Next in the procession comes Ronnie's old blue Ford, its mufflers crackling each time the procession slows. Bunnie has stopped crying and is talking with much animation to Ronnie. She is turned to face him, her back against the door, one leg curled under her on the seat. Ronnie glances repeatedly at the long portions of her stockinged thighs that show below the mini-skirt. She toys with her hair while she talks and makes no effort to pull the skirt down. There are seven other cars strung out behind these. A single sea gull soars soundlessly above as the cars roll past the hilly pastureland on the left and the sloping fields on the right that lead to the river. The road to town has now been plowed clear and only a thin hard film of snow covers the road, melting in spots where salt and chemicals have been scattered by the town trucks. All signs of life beyond the high banks of the road, including the frozen river, are concealed by the unbroken snow. The road begins to wind through the dark section of spruce forest that is dotted with scattered birch trees. The wind has cleared most of the snow from the boughs, but gusts still find pockets among the branches and scatter swirling tendrils. These glitter in the sunlight that here and there falls through the dark tangle of branches. Ronnie and Hank often came here to cut stovewood logs from the pine and from the hardwood patches farther back in the forest.

"She'll put them back in the barn as soon as you leave," Bunnie says, twirling her hair around her left index finger.

"That's all right," Ronnie says. "As long as they were there when that Stevens creep screwed the box shut. Everyone sees them for the last time, including me. Now, as far as I'm concerned, since I won't be back, they will always be there where they belong." He looks quickly at Bunnie's face and she smiles at him. He thinks about how soft she is; how the blond hair around her face and the fuzz on her limbs makes her seem to glow. He glances underneath the mini-skirt at her panty-stockings, sees the point where the legs meet at the top in a heavy seam beneath which is the white of her underpants. This scanning of his sister's body takes a moment and then Bunnie, who has been watching him do it, breaks the silence and says:

"She moved them out of there so fast. Do you know when she did it?"

"She was still up last night when I went to bed. I think she did it then."

"In the dark?"

"I woke up once and saw the yard light on. I thought Boyd was there for one of his *chats*." Ronnie's sarcasm is understood between them. "She must have been lugging trophies then. She could have never done it after the snowfall. It took me six trips to get them back."

"I thought I'd die when she walked in with Grandpa Simmons and saw them."

"Uh-huh. She looked right at Hank like he got up out of the box and put 'em back himself." Ronnie bows his head toward the steering wheel and chuckles. Bunnie collapses on the seat in a fit of laughter. Her hair touches Ronnie's hip and her warm hand rests on his thigh while she laughs. When she sits up there are tears of laughter in her eyes.

"She didn't take out his clothes," Bunnie says.

"Not yet." Ronnie looks at Bunnie's legs as she readjusts her position against the door.

"What do you do with a dead man's clothes?" she asks.

"Give them to the Indians, I guess."

They are laughing when the car tops the hill that overlooks the town. Snow covers the roofs of the stores and houses, the parking lot behind the A&P, the streets, the church, and the cemetery beyond the harbor. Only the ocean is the same: a gray mass stretching out to the clear horizon and dotted by whitecaps pushed up by the fierce wind. There are no boats out, and Ronnie knows that there are small craft or possibly even gale warnings. They fall silent as the procession descends the hill into town. Two men on the main street turn to watch the procession pass. Ronnie cannot see into the restaurant, but he knows there are people seated at the counter who have turned from their lunch to see Hank Mandeville's funeral go by. Ronnie is surprised to see Del Mackenzie pumping gas into a new dark-green Oldsmobile at Boyd's station. He tries to remember what Boyd said about the station being closed. As they cross the turnbridge, he can feel the tidal river rushing below. Two gulls sit on the railing facing the procession, gusts of wind ruffling their white breastfeathers. As Ronnie's car reaches them, one spreads its wings, catches the wind and glides away without a stroke.

At the cemetery Ronnie stands watching absently the casket he has just helped lower onto the snow-covered plot. He wears nothing on his head, and his ears are burning with pain in the frozen wind. Friends and relatives stomp their feet, rub their gloved hands together or cover their ears with their hands or coat collars. Ronnie sniffles and wipes his nose with the back of his glove. The crowd stands in a half-circle around the box while Reverend Sloan says his piece. He can barely be heard against the wind and the sound of the ocean roaring and banging against the rocks not far below the cemetery. Random clouds scud across the sun, casting the scene in a gray light. They pass quickly and the mourners are bathed in the windy winter sunlight again. Ronnie looks among the bowed heads for Bunnie. She is watching him, and when he sees her, she throws her handkerchief up to her mouth to stop her laugh and quickly bows her head. Her shoulders begin to convulse and she looks as if she is crying. Someone touches Ronnie's left elbow and when he turns his head, he sees it is Boyd. With his head bowed but his eyes open, the big man distorts his mouth and whispers: "What's so funny with you and your sister?" Ronnie does not answer. Instead he changes his face from a smile to a frown, and looking out at the violent ocean, moves his elbow so that Boyd's hand falls away, slowly to the floor of the barn.

When Reverend Sloan is finished, there is an awkward pause since there is no hole to lower the casket into. There will be none for another six weeks until the ground thaws enough to dig one. Ronnie was told the casket will be stored but he does not know where. The crowd begins to move away to the cars, and only then does Ronnie notice the two men in heavy wool work-jackets who remain behind. Their pick-up truck is half hidden behind a tool shed in the far corner of the cemetery. Ronnie stops to let the crowd pass. Boyd is helping Virginia Jane back to the station wagon. She is crying, and from the rear she seems aged and bent over like an old crone. Reverend Sloan picks his way over the snow with his right arm extended to brace Grandpa Simmons and his left hand, holding his Bible, also extended for balance. Bunnie is already heading for Ronnie's Ford, swinging her pocketbook and paying less attention to the slippery snow than to the form with which she sways when she walks. Ronnie looks back at the casket. The two workmen are watching the crowd leave. They are smoking and one of them is leaning on the casket. When he sees Ronnie watching him, he stands up.

As he walks to his car, Boyd's station wagon passes him without a glimmer of recognition from any of the stone faces inside except Reverend Sloan who smiles a patient smile with his face turned to the window. When he reaches the car, Bunnie is already seated with her back against the door, arm across the top of the seat, long thin legs showing, smoking a cigarette. Ronnie gets in and slams the door, and she says:

"Go the long way."

She inhales amateurishly, keeping most of the smoke in her mouth. Ronnie starts the car and says nothing to her. As he looks back over his shoulder while the car is rolling in reverse, he sees one of the workmen walking to get the truck. He looks at the casket and at the other workman who has turned away from him, then at Bunnie, who is also looking out the rear window straining the muscles and tendons in her soft, slender neck. His is the last car in the cemetery, and when he turns around and eases it into first gear, the police chief standing out on the road waves him on. He guides the car through the stone gate and uses his turn signal to indicate to the uniformed man that he does not want to turn left like the other ten cars that have preceded him, but wants to go right on the winding road that follows the edge of the ocean. The police chief shifts his position several steps and waves him on in that direction. He nods as Ronnie passes him, but Ronnie cannot see his eyes behind the mirror-front sunglasses.

The letter that Hank takes from the mailbox at the end of the driveway is from the police chief. The day is cold and Hank is wearing only a flannel shirt, but he stands on the edge of the road near the bank of snow and tears open the envelope. It contains a notice authorized by the town's Board of Selectmen requesting him to move the four racing stock cars that sit in various rusted and wheelless postures in the yard and in two of the four stalls of the carriage house that connects the house and the barn.

The cars have not been touched, except to remove parts from them, since Hank's racing career ended three summers before in a motorcycle accident that shattered both his legs in so many places he now walks with a severe body-dipping limp. He was ahead in points for his fifth silver bowl as top driver of the summer at the speedway when he had the accident. The following summer he re-entered racing as a mechanic for another driver, the brother of the man who was killed riding on the motorcycle with him, drinking beer on a warm evening over back country roads.

From the mailbox, Hank returns to the house to get his red wool jacket. He tells Bunnie who is reading in the sunny living room of the house—it is midmorning and the sun falls through the two southern windows—that he needs her help for a moment out in the yard. She sighs with slight annoyance but puts her book down open-faced on the cushion beside her, and, slipping into her loafers, follows him out. She asks him if she needs a jacket, but he says no, he only wants her for a minute, and he goes through the door, limping with determination toward the barn. While she waits outside the barn with her arms folded tightly across her chest in the cold, he drives the pick-up truck from the barn and maneuvers it into position behind the car nearest the barn, a pre-war coupé painted pink with a white 37 on its side and two flat rear tires. When he has the wooden pushing bumper on the front of the truck directly in line with the bumper on the rear of the pink car, he tells Bunnie to get in and steer the car up the wooden ramp into the barn while he pushes it with the truck. When she is finished with her task, she hurries back into the house with her arms again folded across her chest. Hank parks the truck in the yard and returns to the barn.

He positions the car directly under the block and tackle apparatus that is suspended from the central beam of the barn's high roof. In less than an hour, he has the engine disconnected from its mounts, manifold and fuel supply. Connecting it to the thick ropes of the block and tackle, he pulls the length of rope that slowly raises the engine to the level of the windshield of the car. When it is high enough for him to work underneath it, he ties the rope to a vertical beam of one of the animal stalls and leans over the fender into the vacant pit of the engine compartment to check and adjust the car's clutch mechanism. If the rope should break—it is as thick as a woman's wrist—or the knot slip, the falling engine would cut his body in half, crush his skull.

While he is in this defenseless position (one of his racing friends once set his pants on fire as he worked like this in a makeshift garage at a fairground in New Hampshire) his son, Ronnie, drives in and joins him in the barn. Toying with and fixing his old cars is not an unusual thing for Hank to do on a Saturday morning, so Ronnie does not even question why he is there. Instead they talk about Ronnie's fight. There is some ensuing horseplay. Hank jokingly questions Ronnie's fighting ability and Ronnie counters by booting the defenseless mechanic in his exposed backside. They roll on the floor and pretend to pummel each other, and when they stand up out of breath and wheezing with laughter, Hank pulls the police chief's notice from his pocket and shows it to Ronnie.

"Is that why you're fixing this old wreck?" Ronnie asks him. "So you can claim it isn't junk and leave it out there by the road?"

"That's right," Hank puffs. "And I need your help."

"Why not just push it behind the carriage house so nobody can see it when they drive by? They don't say you have to get rid of it, just keep it out of sight."

"But it can be fixed, and we're going to fix all four of them," Hank says.

"You're kidding," Ronnie says. He is astonished but he smiles to show that he is pleased.

"Never. When they come to tell us to get rid of them, we'll drive them around the yard to prove they're not junk."

"What'll you do for parts?"

"Borrow them. I can get any part I want for any car in the state of Maine with just a phone call. It's the dead of winter, and nobody is going to be doing any racing until May. We'll go over to Jimmy Bissonette's place tomorrow and get the engine out of the Chevy he races. And while we're there we might as well take the fuel pump and the radiator. That plus a couple of patched-up tires is all we need for that blue job sitting over by the edge of the house."

Ronnie looks out through the barn doors and across the yard to the powder-blue Mercury sitting with its front end buried in the bank of plowed driveway snow. Virginia Jane has several times complained, but only half-heartedly, about its location. It is sitting in what once was her flower bed at the side of the house. Virginia Jane has had little to say about the yard, even though the property has been in her family for three generations. Her interests have been confined, instead, to the interior of the house, which is kept spotless and polished and rosy. Not one wet boot is allowed beyond the hallway, not one pair of underpants allowed to linger on a bedroom floor, not one particle of dust allowed to fall, although Ronnie, as a child, has seen them, seen them falling through the sunlight that fell through the two southern windows of the living room where he lay on the couch in front of the warm stove with pneumonia and with his secret about his father. He had wondered how Virginia Jane would keep this falling dust from hitting the floor. And he wondered if she would keep Hank from killing his son when he returned with his broken hand healed.

Ronnie looks out at the yard—Hank's domain—that is decorated with junked stock cars and their components. Rusted and sloppily numbered bodies without windows and with intricate tube-braced interiors sit around the yard wearing their scars and bruises, their flattened roofs and chewed fenders, like the trophies on the shelves and mantel in the spotless living room. Engines and transmissions and buckets and pans of blackened bolts and gaskets and lost tools clog the stalls of the open carriage house that stretches between the house and the barn.

"I'm taking your engine for the silver Ford in the carriage house," Hank says. While Ronnie was looking around the yard, Hank had ducked back under the dangling engine.

"What'll I use for a car?" Ronnie asks.

"You can use the truck," Hank answers from the bowels of the pink car.

"How long will it take?" Ronnie asks.

To answer the question, Hank comes back out from under the engine. "For the four of them, we can do it in a week," he says.

"What do you want me to do?" Ronnie asks.

"Start patching and mounting tires," Hank tells him and ducks under the dangling engine again.

"I have to go to work this afternoon at three," Ronnie says.

"Take some wheels with you," Hank says. "I don't think Mr. Boyd'll mind if we use some of his air."

Ronnie's laugh expresses the mutual contempt—although as yet for different reasons—they have for Boyd. This project of fixing cars to beat the town officials and the state law has drawn them together for the moment. Ronnie bends to his task and soon has one of the flat tires from the pink coupé up on the wheel mount in the rear of the barn. In less than half an hour he has the two flat tires from the coupé and three more that were in the barn separated into tires, inner tubes and rims and put into the trunk of his car so he can take them to Boyd's air supply and find their leaks and patch them. He has taken the jack to the carriage house to begin removing flat tires from the silver Ford when he hears Hank call him from the barn. It is nearly lunchtime, and since he is hungry, he thinks his father wants to tell him to break for the noon meal.

The barn smells of grain and gasoline, and he does not see Hank when he enters. He hears his father call again, and when he looks up in the direction of the voice, he sees Hank at the edge of the top loft of the barn, three stories up, holding the ropes from the block and tackle apparatus. He leans slightly out over the edge of the loft and sunlight falls through chinks in the barn roof in the dusty darkness behind him. He shouts down to Ronnie to climb up and give him a hand with one of the ropes that has slipped over the edge of its pulley and jammed on the axle between the pulley's edge and casing. Ronnie shouts back that it is lunchtime, and can't it wait until after they eat. Hank says that the pins in his bad leg hurt and he does not want to have to climb back up to the loft after lunch. Ronnie grumbles but begins to ascend the stairs to the second-floor loft. From that loft to the top loft he must climb a wooden ladder whose rungs are thick hand-hewn boards made before the Civil War. Ronnie is wearing a pair of gloves lined with rabbit fur that make it difficult for him to grip the uneven rungs. Near the top his hand slips from one of them but he manages to re-establish his grip immediately. He looks down and sees that a fall to the second-floor loft would be a dangerous one. Around the base of the ladder is an accumulation of stored furniture—chests, vanities, a variety of kitchen chairs—as well as odd sizes of lumber, a cracked grind wheel and dusty garden tools. He climbs through the square opening at the top of the ladder onto the floor of the top loft. The loft is empty except for some remnants of straw in the corners or trapped between the dark wide boards of the floor, and far back in the shadows the large frame of a curtain stretcher with its many nails protruding and covered with dust. Hank is struggling fiercely with the thick rope, trying to free it. He asks Ronnie to take the other end of it on the opposite side of the pulley. Ronnie must lean out over the edge of the loft to get the rope, and he puts one of his hands against the center beam of the roof as a brace. After he has taken the rope in his hand, he looks down, far down to the floor below. The pink coupé sits calmly, its hood open, its engine compartment empty. The engine rests on its side next to the car, almost in darkness on the opposite side from the barn door through which sunlight is streaming. Together now the two men begin to jerk the trapped rope. The dangling ropes and the apparatus, with its chain free now, begin to dance and sway. The men must lean out over the edge of the loft to do this. The edge of the loft is worn and sagging. The entire barn is falling. It sags toward the creek on its far side. The heavy winter snows will some day force it into that creek. It will sink in jerky stages and then topple quickly in an explosion of dust and snow and dry lumber. Both men are jerking the rope upward, and both use their free hands to brace themselves against the top beam of the barn roof. Holding the trapped rope for balance, Hank reaches for the other ropes to still their jumping. At the same time, Ronnie, who is hungry and annoyed that this little struggle couldn't wait until after lunch, loses his patience and jerks the opposite side of the rope violently. The free ropes swing toward Ronnie and the trapped rope snaps from Hank's grip. Hank is now empty-handed and it seems as if he will be able to lunge back at the boy and onto the worn boards of the loft. He falls down the length of ropes to the floor below. Falls far below. Falls. He strikes the front fender of the pink coupé and slides gently to the floor.

To catch his balance when the rope jerks free from Hank's hand, Ronnie topples back several steps. When he regains his balance, Hank is gone. Instinctively Ronnie drops the rope and back-pedals several steps away from the edge. He drops to a crouch and then falls forward to his knees so he can crawl to the edge of the loft. The ropes are still bouncing and swaying. Ronnie stretches out full length on his stomach and peeks cautiously over the edge of the loft. Hank is sprawled on the floor beside the pink coupé. One of his legs is bent unnaturally under him, and there is blood running swiftly from his nose and mouth. There is also a stain spreading at the crotch of his overalls, but Ronnie does not notice this. Gusts of wind blowing through the barn door flap the collar of Hank's red wool jacket against his jaw. Ronnie continues to stare at the scene from his prone position on the loft floor. The ropes become still. Hank does not move. The blood coming from several orifices in his head—possibly even his ear—flows in a widening puddle around the crumpled body, staining the snow. Falls away to the barn floor. The thick board falls heavily against the hairline. Timmons sits up abruptly and spits a mouthful of blood into the snow. The board strikes down on his upturned face.

Ronnie rolls quickly away from the edge of the loft. He is on his back and he presses his gloved hands together against his chest and squeezes his eyes tightly shut. Bunnie is calling them to come into the house for lunch. She calls several times from the porch steps and then Ronnie can hear her hurrying across the yard, her footsteps squeaking in the frozen snow. Ronnie opens his eyes and stares at the dusty light coming through the chinks between the boards in the barn roof. With his eyes open and concentrating on the dust, the sound of Bunnie's footsteps seem to stop. He has seen dust like this before, falling slowly in the sunlight coming through the two southern windows of the living room. Hank stumbles through the snow to the steps of the porch. He sits near the broken porch rail while he catches his breath. Bunnie's scream smashes against the roof of the barn, shatters and cascades in thousands of glittering pieces down over Ronnie. He does not shut his eyes against it, but instead rolls over and inches his way cautiously, silently to the edge of the loft. Bunnie screams again before he reaches the edge. When he looks over, he sees her far below with her hands locked under Hank's arms, dragging him backwards toward the door. Hank's crumpled leg has straightened out. His head is hanging limp and spilling blood against her left forearm. His eyes appear to be open, but Ronnie cannot tell at this distance. Bunnie drags Hank about halfway to the barn door and then suddenly drops him and screams again. Hank's head bounces against the barn floor. Crumples into the snow, blood gushing from the hairline. Bunnie takes her grip again, her legs backpedaling, and begins her stooping drag of the body once more, but she abandons this almost immediately. The head again thuds against the barn floor. She runs from the barn.

Ronnie is up immediately and rushing dangerously down the hand-hewn ladder. He jumps the last six steps and feels the pain dart up through the muscles of his legs and into his testicles. He takes the steps from the second-floor loft without caution and sprinting across the barn floor, he drops to his knees and skids to Hank's side. Bunnie's panicked efforts to move Hank have smeared the blood that is running from his mouth, nose and one ear across his left cheek and temple and on that side of his forehead. His eyes are open, but Ronnie cannot tell if he is alive. Ronnie jumps to his feet and is about to bolt for the house, but he drops to his knees again and feels for Hank's pulse. He is not sure where on the wrist to find it, so he bends his head to bring his ear next to Hank's nose and mouth. He hears no breathing, so he drops his head to Hank's chest, where he is able to hear what sounds like a heartbeat. His head is still pressed against the chest, and his hands still hold the wrist tightly when Bunnie and Virginia Jane run into the barn.

Bunnie begins to cry again on the drive along the shore road, and Ronnie reaches over and takes her hand and holds it tightly. He doesn't try to say anything to her but instead watches the ocean on his right as it booms into the rocky shore below the stone wall at the road's edge. Waves and spume sometimes leap straight up as high as the wall. There are no birds on the water at all; the black ducks and winter sea ducks have moved into the calmer marshes and only a few gulls play on the wind above the edge of the water. Ronnie looks for boats, perhaps an oil freighter laboring its way through the sunny gale to Portland, but he sees none. There are no fishing boats either in the fierce wind. The road winds in and out to follow the bank as closely as possible. There is no other traffic and the snow here has not been cleared as thoroughly as on the other more frequently traveled roads near town. There are summer homes along both sides of the road, their driveways and lawns and stone walls and rose trellises covered with snow. On the left, away from the ocean, the land becomes scrub woods, an area that was once pine forest reaching to the sea, but which burned several years before and is now a thick tangle of new trees and bushes, competing with each other for root space and sunlight. This woods, where it can be penetrated, yields an extraordinary crop of blueberries in the summertime. The summer residents who live in the large houses bordering the ocean and the road, the houses whose windows are now shuttered and boarded to the sea, pick the berries along the edge of the growth for summer pies. Ronnie and Bunnie have often been into these woods to pick berries for Virginia Jane to can for winter pies and preserves. Bunnie still goes, along the paths she has found alone and along those shown to her by her friends and relatives. Ronnie has not picked berries here since before he went into the Marines three years ago, but now as Bunnie's sobbing begins to subside, he talks nostalgically about their trips into these woods. It is calming for Bunnie to hear about them. She crushes out the cigarette which has burned down while she cried. Freeing her hand from Ronnie's grip, she lights another one. Ronnie now places his free right hand on the wheel, and this time the fresh clouds of smoke tempt him. Perhaps it is the excess of lighting two cigarettes in a row which is tempting. He has not smoked for five months, quitting for his boxing, but he is still tempted. They talk about smoking, and Ronnie tells her how much he would like a cigarette now. Bunnie sits with her back to the door again, rubbing her eyes with the heel of her hand. When Ronnie mentions how wild the ocean looks, she turns to view it and then sits facing straight ahead, smoking her cigarette quickly in the silence that follows his remark. The ocean drive ends and the road winds left into the scrub woods. Bunnie turns back to face Ronnie, tucking her left leg under her right one. The large summer homes with their boarded windows have vanished, and there is now an occasional shack or small house trailer set on a small cleared plot near the edge of the road. The road will eventually come to a fork. The right fork will lead to the next fishing village along the ocean, and the left will follow the river several miles upstream until it crosses a bridge behind the Mandeville farm. Near that bridge, but before they leave the woods, Ronnie stops the car and pulls it as close as he can to the snow bank along its edge.

"I don't feel like going back yet," he explains to Bunnie, who nods and continues to puff on her cigarette.

The sun warms the car, and there is little need for the heater, so Ronnie shuts off the car motor. Almost as soon as it stops, they can hear the raucous blue jays feeding in the woods.

"What do they do with the casket?" he asks after a moment.

"I don't know," his sister answers and turns her back to the door again and spreads her left leg out over the space between them on the seat. She reaches behind her back and rolls the window down several inches and drops the stub of her cigarette over her shoulder and out onto the snowbank. Incredibly, she lights a third and rolls the window back up.

"Give me a cigarette," Ronnie says. He can stand the temptation no longer. She hands him one and he places the filter end of it between his teeth. He continues to look out through the windshield with both hands under the suède skirt he slowly rolls her tights and underwear down over the slight bulge of her white hips. Bracing herself against the door, Bunnie raises her buttocks slightly to assist him. When he has rolled them free of her buttocks, she sits again and he pulls the rolls of garments down along her smooth thighs to her knees. She slouches to assist the entry of her brother's index and middle fingers into the damp warmth between her legs. With the match cupped in both hands, Ronnie lights the cigarette. He does not inhale because the clouds of smoke in the car now irritate him instead of tempting him. He rolls his window down slightly because the glass is beginning to fog. He drops the dead match over the edge of the glass.

"This is terrible," he says to her, looking at the cigarette burning between his fingers.

"Throw it out if you don't want it," she answers. She tucks her leg under her and laughs at his attempt to smoke. "Inhale," she urges. Ronnie takes another puff and tries to draw the smoke into his lungs, but he coughs it up immediately and his sister laughs even harder. He drops the burning cigarette over the edge of the glass and rolls the window up again.

"I'm supposed to ask you not to fight tonight," Bunnie says suddenly. She has stopped laughing.

"You too?" Ronnie says without surprise.

"So, consider yourself asked," she says and smiles when he looks over at her.

"The three of you will make a good team. Mr. and Mrs. Boyd and their daughter, Bernice."

"Oh, come on," Bunnie says nervously.

"'My, that was a fine sermon this morning, Reverend Sloan,'" Ronnie mocks in a mincing falsetto.

"Isn't he awful?" Bunnie asks, referring to the preacher who has just eulogized Hank.

"He didn't even know Hank, and he probably didn't care. While that crap was rolling out of his mouth, I kept hearing Hank say: 'Bullshit. Bullshit. All bullshit!' That's why I was laughing at the cemetery."

Bunnie smiles at this scoffing vision of Hank that Ronnie has conjured up, but a sudden tear plunges down each of her cheeks.

"Is he like that in church too?" Ronnie continues.

"Yes," Bunnie answers. "I wouldn't go if Mother didn't make me." She lowers her eyes because she knows this is a lie. She would go, because she believes in God. Believes in God the way she believes in horses and movie stars and her high school basketball team.

"And Mother wouldn't go if Boyd didn't make *her*," Ronnie says and laughs. "The preacher was Boyd's idea."

"But she wanted one too," Bunnie insists. "Anyway, how can you have a funeral without a preacher?"

"I don't know. Have a friend say something. Or just put him in the hole and cover him up."

A sob explodes from Bunnie. Ronnie does not want to be cruel to her, so he reaches for her hand to comfort her. In doing this, he bumps her cigarette and knocks off its burning head. He draws back his burned hand, and Bunnie stiffens her body and begins to beat around her clothes searching for the live coal. Ronnie sees smoke rising from the crack in the seat, and he slides his hand in and knocks out the coal, brushes it to the floor and steps on it. Bunnie relights the half-smoked cigarette in silence. Through the windshield they can see a gray squirrel venture haltingly along the road toward the car. When it has almost reached them, Ronnie turns on the ignition and presses the horn. The squirrel bounds indignantly in an explosion of snow up over the plowed bank at the side of the road. Ronnie continues to sound the horn until the animal has scrambled up an oak tree and out of sight across a network of branches in a panic of falling dead leaves and snow. He laughs harshly and Bunnie forces a smile. There is a short silence and then she says:

"It was horrible, Ronnie." The tears appear again on the cheeks she has just wiped dry. "I'll see him laying there for the rest of my life. And smell that smell." Ronnie moves to her. She begins to sob on his shoulder. "I didn't know what to do with him, so I dragged him. I don't know why. I don't know why." When she has sobbed it out and is more quiet, she says, with her head still resting on his shoulder: "If only you'd been there, I'm sure it wouldn't have happened."

"Probably not," Ronnie says, looking out at the snow-covered road through windows that are beginning to fog. "Probably not." He thinks of telling her that he was there; that somehow he is responsible. That it wasn't her father after all that he killed; just her mother's husband. But he is not sure that he did kill him, not sure he was even there and not out in the yard as he told them when it happened, not sure that Carl Timmons is her father, or that Hank killed Carl Timmons, who seven years ago was a night watchman in an amusement park in California, or that Hank even tried to kill Timmons, because no one has ever told him these things. And then, too, he is put off from his secrets—this murder, that murder, his father, her father—by her scream shattering against the roof of the barn and cascading in glittering pieces of snow down over him as he lies on the floor of the loft. He crawls, looks over, sees her far below with her hands locked under Hank's arms. He strokes her blond hair until she sits up and examines her inflamed eyes in the rear-view mirror. She is not satisfied with her appearance, but he has already started the car. "Let's get back," she says hoarsely.

In addition to the driveway, Boyd has cleared the

snow away from a section of the yard so additional cars can be parked there. He is just finishing when Ronnie pulls up into the space that has just been plowed. Boyd steps out of his jeep at the same moment that Bunnie and Ronnie get out of the Ford, and there is the sound of three car doors slamming almost simultaneously. The wind has stopped for the moment and the sky is becoming more overcast.

"Hi kids," Boyd says. "Where have you been?"

Bunnie pauses and answers: "We took the long way up the river road." Ronnie walks straight for the house without breaking his stride. Boyd stares at his departing back and then motions Bunnie on, saying: "You go ahead, honey. I'm going to get some more salt for those steps." Bunnie lowers her eyes and turns away from him, and Boyd heads for the barn. Bunnie walks several steps and then runs to catch up with Ronnie.

"Do you have any gum?" she asks him, taking his arm to keep from slipping on the icy snow. "I must smell like a smokestack."

Ronnie shakes his head to indicate that he has no chewing gum. His hands are jammed tightly in his pockets, and he moves his elbow away from his body to accommodate Bunnie's grip on his arm.

"There's no ice on these steps," Ronnie says as they walk up onto the porch. The steps are wet from the salt that was put on them by Boyd before they left for the funeral. In spots the sun and wind have dried the water and left a thin pattern of white crust from the dissolved salt. "Why does he have to be such a fussy pain in the ass?" Ronnie continues as he holds open the front door for Bunnie. Bunnie lowers her eyes in embarrassment because Virginia Jane is standing just inside the door talking with her cousin, Mildred Tupper, and the woman's husband, who is a lobsterman. It is obvious that they have heard Ronnie's remark. Bunnie says hello and nods her head several times to keep from looking at them. When she gets past them she hurries down the hall to the bathroom. Ronnie, one of his hands still deep in his pocket and the other trying to pull the door shut, mumbles a greeting to them and walks past headed toward the kitchen. He has not shut the door tightly enough, however, and a gust of wind draws it wide open and slams it against the wall of the house. The people in the hallway stare at Ronnie without moving, and he must come back between them to close the door properly. Just before he pulls it shut, he sees Boyd striding across the yard from the barn with a coffee can full of rock salt.

It is lunchtime and Ronnie is hungry. This will be his last chance to eat until after his fight that evening. The fight is the longest he has ever had—six three-minute rounds—and it is against the best opponent he has ever had except during his company's matches in the Marines when he was overmatched several times and had to take severe beatings. He is more concerned about saving face tonight than he is about winning. There is little chance that he will win, but if he can last through six rounds without getting sick or too badly beaten, he will consider it an accomplishment. His opponent is mediocre but professional, and Ronnie is less than mediocre. He was chosen for this fight as a last-minute substitute, the only one available in his particular weight class.

In the kitchen, one of his cousins, a child wearing a shiny blue suit, is standing on tiptoe, reaching up over the edge of the sink to draw himself a glass of water from the faucet. Ronnie does not speak to him but goes directly to the refrigerator, and finds a large serving bowl filled with lobster salad and two more filled with potato salad. There are also several trays containing cold cuts and cheeses. The entire bottom shelf is taken up by cans of beer and soft drinks. Ronnie rolls up a slice of boiled ham and slips it into his mouth, and while he is chewing this, Virginia Jane comes down the hall and into the kitchen with several guests.

"Stay out of that until it's served," she says to him, and they pass into the dining room.

The boy at the sink has finished his water. He puts the glass on the drainboard and looks over at Ronnie to see what he will do. Ronnie keeps stuffing large hunks of the cold lobster into his mouth. He shuts the refrigerator door when his mouth is so full he can barely chew. The boy goes out of the kitchen and Virginia Jane returns alone.

"What are you eating now?" she asks him, annoyed.

Ronnie opens his mouth wide to show her the semi-masticated mass of lobster and mayonnaise, and she turns away in disgust. He walks past her to the stove and lifts the lid on a large kettle filled with hot clam chowder.

"Please wait until things are served," she pleads in exasperation. He replaces the kettle lid slowly and says through his mouthful of lobster:

"O.K., O.K."

"Where's Bernice?" she asks him, moving up beside him. Ronnie nods in the direction of the bathroom and begins to walk away from her toward the dining room.

"Wait," she says. "Take this." Hurriedly she fills a serving tray with beer and soda cans from the refrigerator and gives it to Ronnie. "Put it next to the glasses on the buffet," she says. Ronnie turns to go again, and again she says: "Wait," and draws from the refrigerator a silver bowl filled with ice cubes. "Take this too."

Ronnie balances the tray with one hand and takes the bowl in his other. He turns to go out with his load, and she says: "Put the ice next to the liquor." Still chewing, Ronnie nods and walks into the dining room. He can hear Virginia Jane calling Bunnie to help serve the food, and then suddenly she is beside him again as he passes the dining-room table. "Mix drinks for people," she whispers in his ear, "just to get them started."

"I'm hungry," Ronnie protests, but she waves him on and hurries back to the kitchen.

While Ronnie is mixing whiskey and ginger ale and opening beers for the relatives and sodas for their children, he sees Boyd through one of the dining-room windows. The big man has finished sprinkling the unnecessary salt, and he is putting the coffee can out of sight beside the porch steps. When he comes onto the porch and reaches for the door, Ronnie moves several steps to his right so he can see Virginia Jane come to the door to greet him. They embrace quickly, and Boyd removes his light tan cowboy hat before he leans down to give Ronnie's mother a kiss on the cheek.

Carl Timmons leans down sweetly to kiss Virginia Jane Simmons on the cheek. They are at a class picnic at Bear Lake. He is also holding one of her hands. She faces the camera, smiling shyly; he is in profile, his lips puckered. The focus of the photograph is blurred, and the reproduction in the 1944 *Abnaki,* their high school yearbook, further distorts it. The caption beneath reads: "Caught in the Act!" Ronnie, sweating from the aspirin his mother has given him, looks up from his pillow-propped position on the couch in the hot living room and sees dust falling through the sunlight that falls through the two southern windows. All that remains of his pneumonia is a cough and this constant perspiration. "Puppy Love?" reads the caption under the picture of the two of them holding hands, standing on the sidelines at a fall football game. They are unaware of the camera here and are watching the action in front of them. Ronnie is seven years old. He knows this dead man, who, in the picture, is just a boy in blue jeans and flannel shirt, holding Virginia Jane's hand. Outside, the snow rises to the sills of the sunlit windows, and it is almost a year that Hank has been gone. Ronnie sometimes thinks that Hank has been taken and executed for the murder of Carl Timmons, who is just a boy in the yearbook pictures Ronnie holds in his lap. Just a boy as Ronnie is a boy. But if Hank is still a fugitive, will he want to return and silence the only witness to his crime: the boy, Ronnie?

The perspiration on Ronnie's forehead is from the aspirin his mother has given him.

But these thoughts have little reality for Ronnie. They are from a comic book world and mingle with the exaggerated posturings of two-dimensional villains and their righteous nemeses. What *does* have substance for Ronnie is the ache he feels when he thinks that Hank may never return. He tries not to think about Hank because when this ache comes to him, he can shed it only in sleep or in some distracting physical activity. But now, confined to the couch in this hot living room, it is something that is constantly with him. He feels helpless without Hank, unable to do the things that he enjoyed doing with his father: the motorcycle rides, clinging with fright and joy to his father's strong back while the wind tore tears from his eyes; sitting on the cold concrete floor of the Chevy garage arranging a disarray of old bolts and spark plugs and lug nuts into a magical town of streets and houses and people and cars while the whine and roar of the repair work broke in on the easy conversation and laughter of the mechanics. Now he is lost in this house of women and old people. His grandfather is teaching him to play a violin; his baby sister cries and vomits throughout the day and night. His mother has thrown away all his blue jeans and he now wears good woolen pants to school which he rips and is scolded for.

There is no caption under the picture of Virginia Jane and Carl Timmons smiling broadly, uncontrollably pressed cheek-to-cheek sitting on the hay in the large wagon used for the class hayride. This too is in the fall section of the book, an entire page of snapshots of various members of the class who participated in the ride. In the pictures the day is very sunny. It is early fall and the leaves are still on the trees. The air looks hazed and warm. Perhaps this is what one expects from the sunlight reflecting on the hay. Virginia Jane's hair is frizzed. She wears a print dress. Carl Timmons wears overalls. His hair is long and slicked into a high pompadour. In the section of senior pictures closer to the front of the book, his hair is chopped off into a crewcut, no doubt in sympathy with the boys overseas. The notes under the picture reveal that he is going to be a fighter pilot for the Army Air Corps, provided "that certain someone" will wait for him. Two pages back it is reported "that certain someone" will bide her time waiting for the handsome fighter pilot by becoming an Army nurse. The book was printed in June of 1944. There are far fewer pages and pictures than usual because of the paper shortage. But Virginia Jane was not permitted by her father to become a nurse, either for the war effort or at home. Instead, she defied Grandpa Simmons by running away and becoming a USO hostess in Pensacola, Florida. This is where Ronnie was born in December of 1945. The war was over.

"I'm anxious to talk to you about the war," Grandpa Simmons says to Ronnie at the buffet where Ronnie is pouring Scotch over ice cubes in a small glass for him.

Ronnie is watching the level of the Scotch carefully and asks:

"What?"

"The war," the tiny tan man repeats. He confronts Ronnie at the drink table, his age-blotched hands folded over his cane, his expensive gray suit shimmering in the light from the ceiling lamp dangling over the dining-room table. "I'm anxious to hear what's really going on over there in those jungles from someone who's been there." He holds up a warning hand. "No water, please. I like it straight. On ice. With a lemon peel."

"There's no lemon," Ronnie says, putting down the pitcher of water that he was about to tilt over Grandpa Simmons' glass. "Mom might have one in the ice box."

"Don't bother," Grandpa Simmons says. "It's fine like this." He picks up the drink and sips from it. "I imagine it's quite a bit different from my war or even your father's," he continues, grimacing at the taste of the drink.

The red face of cousin Harry Fry appears behind Grandpa Simmons.

"Want a drink, Harry?" Ronnie says over his grandfather's shoulder.

"No, Jesus," the voluble lobsterman says. "If I drink that stuff, I'll never see suppertime. Just give me a beer."

Ronnie pulls the ring on the top of one of the cold beer cans and snaps it open. He hands the beer past Grandpa Simmons who is still facing him.

"Don't need the glass," Harry Fry says, holding up a warning hand. "How are you, Uncle Edward?" Harry says before he turns away with his beer.

"Fine. Just fine," the old man replies, turning his head to the side and then turning it back to face Ronnie. When Harry Fry is gone, he says: "How come Harry

Fry never went in the Army? A big young man like that."

"Three kids," Ronnie answers.

Grandpa Simmons takes another sip of his drink and says:

"What's really going on over there? Why don't we just clean up that mess and get out?"

Ronnie shrugs his shoulders. He slides the ice-cube bowl down the buffet to an uncle who is mixing himself a drink. There are twelve other people in the dining room in addition to Ronnie and his grandfather. They are mostly relatives and close friends of the family, and the men in this room and among the twenty or so guests that can be heard in buzzing conversation in the living room represent a cross-section of the small community's occupations, from farmers and fishermen to lawyers and real estate agents. The clothes of the men vary from flannel shirts and old shiny suits dragged out for funerals and weddings to the more fashionable cut of the younger businessmen. It is harder to differentiate among the women, especially since all are wearing dark funeral clothes. The folding chairs that line the edge of the room are borrowed from Reverend Sloan's church, and were picked up by Ronnie and Boyd last night in Boyd's truck. There are no chairs at the dining-room table. The surface of the table has been cleared for the food that will be served buffet-style to the guests. Three leaves have been added to the center of the table so that its shape is approximately the same as the rectangular room. Virginia Jane has already brought out the silverware, plates and napkins and placed them at the far end of the table away from the kitchen.

"What branch?" Grandpa Simmons asks Ronnie.

"Pardon?" Ronnie does not understand the question.

"What branch of the service were you in? I've forgotten. Army?"

"Marines," Ronnie answers. He is distracted and is watching Bunnie come into the room carrying a bowl of potato salad. She has removed the coat to her suit, and he is watching the shape of the gold sweater and the very small, very tight skirt. Bunnie stretches her neck—she is tall for her age and her neck is long and slender—so she can see her body in the medicine cabinet mirror. Her small breasts are naked and she wears white wool socks.

"How long were you there?"

"Thirteen months."

Bunnie puts the bowl down, turns and leaves the room. Ronnie looks at his grandfather.

"What sort of action did you see?" the old man persists.

Hank never asked Ronnie questions about the war. Ronnie had arrived home in the early spring not quite a year ago. A neighbor picks him up as he stands hitchhiking at the spot on Route One where the Bangor bus has dropped him off. It is an overcast and thawing day, working itself slowly into a cold rain. Raw mist and fog hang over the patches of snow in the fields as Ronnie is driven the last few miles to his home. Hank is at work in the barn. Ronnie can see him stand and turn from the spread of engine parts on the barn floor that he has been examining under the glare of a naked light bulb. The neighbor's car pulls across the gravel of the driveway and turns up the road, back toward Route One. Ronnie feels self-conscious in his uniform, wrinkled now from the long bus ride. He walks across the yard carrying his duffle bag. Hank watches him come, and when they stand facing each other in the dim chill of the barn, Hank stretches out his hand and says:

"Are you home for good?"

"Yes," Ronnie answers. "Didn't you get my letter? I said I was getting discharged."

"Yes," Hank says. "But sometimes they get you drunk and talk you into signing up again."

"Not me. I wouldn't want to go back there for a million bucks."

"No. I guess you wouldn't."

The following summer, last summer, Ronnie is dressed to go to the beach for the afternoon. It is his day off from work at Boyd's gas station, a job he had been given shortly after his return. He is dressed in sneakers, a bathing suit and a sweatshirt. Hank is sitting at the kitchen table drinking a can of beer as Ronnie comes down the back stairs from his room, carrying his wallet, a pack of cigarettes and his car keys. Virginia Jane is out working in her garden.

In the kitchen Ronnie walks to the refrigerator and bends into it, looking for something cold to drink.

"What's that?" Hank asks.

Ronnie turns and sees his father pointing to the reddish-purple scar on his hip that extends just below his bathing suit.

"A scar," Ronnie answers, taking out a carton of milk and moving to the sink for a glass.

"Is there more to it?" Hank asks.

Ronnie puts the milk carton on the sink and tugs his bathing suit up to expose six more inches of the ugly scar, fatter at the top end than the bottom.

"How'd you get that?" Hank asks.

Ronnie carefully eases the suit down over the sensitive area and pours himself a glass of milk.

"Piece of a shell," he says.

Hank winces, and Ronnie is surprised to see him show concern.

"It must have hurt like hell," Hank says.

"It didn't break the bone," Ronnie tells him and gulps

down the milk. "Another piece hit me on the helmet and knocked me cold. I didn't even hear it go off. Put a big dent in the helmet and made a mess down here." He points to the hip.

"Oh," Hank says. He looks away from the ugly scar.

Hank asks him nothing more about the war.

"Do you know what they do with caskets?" Ronnie asks Grandpa Simmons.

"Where? Over there?" the old man says, confused.

"No. Here. Hank's casket."

"Why . . . I don't know," Grandpa Simmons replies. "Keep them somewhere, I imagine. Probably in one of the vaults, or maybe even at the undertaker's. I never really thought about it before."

Bunnie comes back into the room with another bowl of potato salad.

"Want some help?" Ronnie asks her.

She looks at him carefully before putting her bowl down. Then she glances at Grandpa Simmons and answers: "Sure."

"Excuse me," Ronnie tells his grandfather and follows her out to the kitchen.

He returns carrying a bowl of lobster salad, trailed by Bunnie carrying a plate of cold cuts. Grandpa Simmons is pouring himself another drink. He turns to face Ronnie, but Ronnie goes back to the kitchen with Bunnie. On the way, they pass Virginia Jane who is carrying a pot of hot coffee out to the buffet table. Alone in the kitchen, Ronnie takes his sister's arm and says quickly:

"I've got to get upstairs and get some sleep or I won't last one round tonight. Will you bring me a ham sandwich and some lobster and a glass of milk, so I don't have to go in there and talk to anybody anymore?"

"Sure." She smiles at him.

"Thanks." He turns and hurries up the back stairs before Virginia Jane returns.

His bedroom is no longer cold. The hot stove below in the living room and the sunlight that fell earlier through the two southern windows have warmed it. The day is fully overcast now and there is no sunlight. Without undressing, Ronnie sprawls on the bed and rolls over on his back. He places his hands behind his head and relaxes, staring at the familiar patterns in the plaster of the ceiling. It is not long before he hears footsteps on the rear stairs. He turns his head to the side and sees Bunnie enter his room. She is carrying a plate in each hand. A glass of milk is balanced next to the pile of lobster salad on the plate in her left hand. On the other plate is a ham sandwich and a fork. A paper napkin is tucked under the edge of the sandwich. When she sees that Ronnie has exposed himself, she stops short and releases her grip on both plates, which fall slowly from her hands to the floor far below. She rushes to the bed. The pieces of each of the breaking plates spring up slowly from the wide floorboards. After their first high bounce, the pieces bound and roll gently away in all directions. Some tumble a great distance across the floor. The milk-coated pieces of the glass do not bounce as much as the pieces of plate. Instead, the glass, which falls almost directly upright, collapses downward into a spread-out pile. The milk splashes up in an almost perfect circular thin sheet. The top edge of this circle is ringed with drops of various sizes, some springing away from it and others remaining attached like milk tears. This ordered pattern settles into a puddle that spreads randomly around the floor. The dense and adhesive lobster salad drops in a clump and lies there. The sandwich lands on its edge and wobbles a few inches before splitting. One of the slices of bread flops to the floor, mustard side up, while the other draped with ham rolls on a few more inches before it stops. The fork lands on its tines and bounds high into the air. It takes two more smaller bounces, rolls over once and lands with its tines up near the foot of the bed. All these pieces—the shattering plates and glass, the splashing milk, the pile of lobster salad, the two slices of bread (one with mustard, one without), the ham and the bouncing fork—come to rest and are motionless in their haphazard positions around the floor before the napkin, which floats in slow pendulous descending arcs, reaches the floor. The napkin comes to rest unfolded one time in a collapsing tent shape with a corner touching the edge of the pile of lobster salad nearest the door. Ronnie does not flinch as his sister throws herself on the exposed lower half of his body, even when she violently slides her arms under his buttocks and grips him tightly enough to lift the middle portion of his body away from the bed in a stiff arc. His head remains on the pillow, but he reaches his arms down and takes the sides of her blond head in his hands as it bobs frantically up and down. After a moment, she becomes more relaxed and her head begins to slide in an easy rhythmic motion. She keeps her firm grasp with her encircled arms, but she allows his buttocks to return slowly to the bed as her head falls with it. Ronnie toys with her long blond hair, twisting it around his fingers and then spreading it out over his naked stomach. He spreads and smooths it in a circle coming from her slowly bobbing head, so that when he raises his head from the pillow to look down at her, all he sees is golden hair pouring over his stomach, hips and thighs. Rising. And falling. He sits up on the edge of the bed before she reaches him and takes the glass from one of the plates that she offers. Smoothing back his hair with his free hand, he places the glass on the floor and then takes the plate with the sandwich, napkin and fork and puts it beside himself on the bed. The plate with the lobster salad he takes last, balancing it on his knees. He begins to eat immediately and Bunnie sits beside him on the edge of the bed.

"Have you eaten yet?" he asks her, jamming a forkful of lobster salad into his mouth.

"No," she answers and then adds: "Well, I picked a little while I was getting yours."

"Here," Ronnie says with his mouth full. He spears a large piece of lobster meat—an entire claw—and separates it from the pile. When she has opened her mouth as wide as she can—she squints her eyes to do this—he stuffs the claw in and withdraws the fork. Mayonnaise comes off on the sides of her mouth and upper lip, and while she is struggling to chew this large bite, she reaches across Ronnie's lap for the napkin.

When she is able to make herself understood, she asks:

"When are you leaving?"

Ronnie pauses, removes the corner of the sandwich from his mouth and says:

"As soon as I get some sleep." He bites into the sandwich.

"Take me with you," Bunnie asks him, turning to look at his face. She places her hand on his mid-thigh causing Ronnie to flinch just the slight amount needed to upset the balance of the lobster salad plate on his knee. Ronnie steadies the plate, and she does not remove her hand. He can feel its warmth through his suit pants. Ronnie chews while she waits patiently for his answer.

"But I'm not going anywhere. After the fight, I'll probably get a hotel room, and then tomorrow I'll find an apartment and look for a job." He takes another bite.

Ronnie wants to be free of any sort of attachment or obligation when he leaves the house. He may or may not get the hotel room after the fight, depending on how tired he is, but he has no intention of staying in Portland, Maine, beyond the next day. After the fight—win or lose—he will receive one hundred dollars for his efforts. He intends to use that money to get himself to a place where there is no snow. He is thinking of New Orleans. It will be Mardi Gras in several weeks. Or Miami. Los Angeles is another possibility, but he is not sure the car or the money will make it that far. But this is his secret—one more secret—from his sister. He will write to her and explain. He will send for her if she cannot tolerate this life. But right now he must get away with no complications.

"You could drop me off," she says to him. "I only want to go to Portland."

He is raising a forkful of lobster salad to his mouth. "You mean you just want a ride to Portland?"

"Yes," she answers.

"Oh," he says through the mouthful of food. "I thought you wanted to go with me."

"Where are you going?"

"Nowhere." He chews and swallows. "What are you going to do in Portland?"

"I have to meet someone there tonight," she answers. "I'll be there at five o'clock. Too early for you?"

"I can wait around."

"Who are you meeting?"

Bunnie looks down at the ball of napkin in her hand and says: "A friend."

"What's his name?" Ronnie asks.

"You don't know him. He's from South Portland."

"What's his name?" Ronnie persists.

"You're as bad as Mother," Bunnie says. She tells Ronnie the boy's name. Ronnie does not know him.

"How old is he?" Ronnie asks.

"Nineteen," Bunnie replies.

"Where did you meet him?"

"At a basketball game."

"Is he still in high school?"

"No. He quit." She is exasperated at his questions and says: "Honestly. You sound just like Virginia Jane."

"Does she know you're going?" Ronnie asks.

"She wouldn't let me go out because it's the day of the funeral," Bunnie tells him. She confides this because she feels Ronnie is her ally in helping to deceive their mother.

"Then you shouldn't go," he tells her.

"You must be kidding," she says.

"Don't you have school tomorrow?" he asks.

"She wants me to stay home one more day," Bunnie tells him.

"Well, if you're going to stay home from school to mourn Hank, you're certainly not going out tonight." Ronnie has stopped eating and is looking at her with a fierce expression.

"What is this?" she shouts at him. "You're going out. You're fighting. You're going away for good. All I want to do is go to a dance."

"Well, you're not going," he tells her flatly. "Not in my car." He takes the last bite of the sandwich.

"You sonofabitch," she shouts and stands up with her fists clenched.

"Watch your mouth," he tells her. His own mouth is filled with sandwich.

"I'm going to tell her that you're leaving," Bunnie says. She bends down and pulls the suitcase from under the bed. "I'm going to show her this."

Ronnie is startled by her shouting, but when he sees the suitcase, he pushes her away from it. She catches her balance and does not fall, and then turns and goes to the door.

"I'm going to tell right now," she says over her shoulder as she leaves the room.

Ronnie, still seated on the edge of the bed, gulps down the full glass of milk. He puts the empty glass and plates beside the bed, pushes the suitcase back into its hiding place, and lies back to look again at the plaster patterns on the ceiling.

Drowsiness overcomes him almost immediately in the warm room. His eyes close and he relaxes for the first time since dawn. He is close to sleep when he hears someone on the back stairs. The footsteps startle him but he does not move or open his eyes. He expects Virginia Jane or perhaps Bunnie again, but these footsteps are heavy. They complete the stairs, pause at his door and enter the room. Still Ronnie does not open his eyes. The steps stop at the bed, and then Ronnie hears his suitcase being dragged out of its hiding place. Without changing his position, he opens his eyes and sees Boyd, crouched down and reaching under the bed. The big man's light, short-cropped hair is only inches from Ronnie's face, so Ronnie speaks softly:

"What are you doing, Boyd?"

Boyd pulls the suitcase all the way out from under the bed and stands up.

"Where do you think you're going?"

"I asked you first," Ronnie says. "What are you doing with the suitcase?"

"Pulling it out so you can unpack it," Boyd says sternly.

"Oh Jesus Christ." Ronnie rolls over so that his back is turned to Boyd towering over the bed.

"You watch your language," Boyd tells him.

"Watch your own fucking language," Ronnie screams at him and sits up quickly on the edge of the bed. His face is red with rage and his fists are clenched. "You think you can come into *my* fucking room UNinvited, and pull out *my* fucking suitcase, and tell *me* to watch *my* fucking language. You get your miserable cocksucking ass the fuck out of my motherfucking room, right fucking now. RIGHT FUCKING NOW."

Boyd stumbles backwards several steps. It seems for a moment as if he will rush at Ronnie.

"———" His mouth opens but he can say nothing.

"Go ahead. Get out. I want to get some sleep, and I don't want every dumb sonofabitch in the county coming in this fucking room. OUT." He stands up and points to the door. He is aware of the urge Boyd has to throttle him. He is provoking it, and he stands up to be prepared to defend himself against it. He watches Boyd clenching and unclenching his fists, opening and closing his mouth.

"I . . . I'm . . ."

"You are not my daddy, Boyd. And you never will be."

"I'm sorry, Ronnie," Boyd says, regaining some composure.

"You have no right to come in here and take things out from under my bed."

"I'm sorry. It was my mistake." Boyd is calm again. "Your mother wanted me to come up and see if I could persuade you not to leave," he continues.

"Christ, you're off on the wrong foot, Boyd. You should have told her to do it herself. Hank would have told her to go fuck herself." He pauses and then adds: "Why didn't she ask me herself?"

"Well, I don't know, Ronnie. I think she's afraid of you."

Ronnie drops, bouncing, into a sitting position on the edge of the bed. He looks at the floor between his feet, but holds his palms up to show that he is perplexed, and says: "She shouldn't be afraid of me. Why is she afraid of me? I wouldn't hurt her." His voice is soft, with a slightly hurt tone.

"She says you threatened her when she came up here to ask you not to fight tonight."

"I didn't threaten her." Ronnie looks up at Boyd for some sign of reassurance.

"There are other things, too," Boyd says, pressing for the upper hand.

"What?" Ronnie asks, still looking up at him.

"The trophies," Boyd says coolly.

"But she put them out in the barn," Ronnie says, the pitch of his voice rising in exasperation.

"She felt they didn't look right for the funeral."

"Oh, hell," Ronnie says, looking back down at his feet.

"She thinks you're mocking her and trying to make a joke out of this. The trophies aren't all. She thinks you dropped the coffin on purpose."

"I didn't drop the damn coffin," Ronnie shouts and stands up angrily. "Somebody slipped, and it wasn't me. For all I know it might have been you."

"It wasn't me," Boyd says.

"Do you think I did it?" Ronnie asks, poking his own chest violently with his thumb.

"Don't get excited," Boyd says. "I didn't say it was you."

Ronnie sits down again, and there is silence for a moment before Boyd says:

"And she thinks you built the fire up so the room would be too hot. And so he'd . . ."

"Smell?" Ronnie begins to laugh, falling backwards on the bed.

"I'm just telling you what she thinks," Boyd says.

"For Christ sake," Ronnie says, cutting off his laughing abruptly and swinging his feet up on the bed. He stares at the ceiling for a moment and then says: "Why don't you get on out of here now?"

Boyd remains standing on the spot he has been on throughout the entire conversation. He says: "I know you can't do anything about getting out of that fight tonight. . . ."

"I don't want to get out of it," Ronnie interrupts.

Boyd ignores him and continues: "But I want to know what you intend to do after the fight."

"Probably get drunk," Ronnie says.

"I mean about coming home."

"I'll worry about that after I get drunk."

"You know I don't want you to leave, Ron," Boyd says with a sudden intimacy. "You know what I told you this morning about my plans for you and that station."

Ronnie turns his head to look at Boyd. "How come that station was open when we drove past it on the way to the cemetery? You told me you were closing it for the funeral."

"Del MacKenzie called me and said he wanted to work. He said he needed the money." Boyd is apologetic.

"You sure you didn't call him?" Ronnie taunts. "I mean those extra three hours' revenue could be important for your cattle plans."

"The man wanted the wages," Boyd says flatly.

"Are you going to pay me for the days I took off for the funeral?" Ronnie asks.

"Certainly," Boyd tells him.

"Why don't you give it to me now?" Ronnie's head is still on the pillow, turned to look at Boyd.

Boyd is speechless again, but he withdraws his wallet from his rear pocket.

"Three days pay comes to about forty dollars," Ronnie says. "There's some extra change, but I'll settle for forty."

Boyd looks in his wallet, but then says: "I can't do it."

"Don't you have it on you?" Ronnie asks. "Then let's drive down to the station since it's open and get it."

"It'll be in your paycheck Friday," Boyd tells him. "I can't give you cash. I'll have no record of it." Boyd turns to leave the room. Ronnie calls his name, and he stops in the doorway and turns around.

"Do you know where they keep Hank's casket until the ground thaws?" Ronnie asks him.

"No," Boyd says and turns and goes down the back stairs.

The room is quiet now and the murmuring and clinking sounds of the guests downstairs seem remote and muted. Although Ronnie is almost certain that someone else, particularly Virginia Jane, will come to his room, he has no trouble relaxing. He begins to doze as soon as Boyd has left the room. He fights this for a few minutes expecting to hear his mother's footsteps on the back stairs. When he forces his eyes open, he can see the fine jagged cracks in the stained plaster of the ceiling. His eyes sting if he watches the ceiling too long, and he must close them frequently to soothe them. Finally, he succumbs to the temptation and voluntarily closes his eyes. He goes easily into sleep. He does not dream.

The voice Ronnie hears is his mother's. She is speaking softly and for a moment he thinks that she is in his room and is speaking to him. He is not aware of how much time has passed, and the weight of sleep is too heavy on him to permit him to open his eyes and search out the clock. As he listens, he realizes that she is in her own room down the hall where Hank's bed is still freshly made. She is speaking to her father. Ronnie can hear the gentle tinkle of ice in Grandpa Simmons' glass as she talks. He fights the sleep but it begins to overtake him again. Virginia Jane is talking about Boyd. She tells Grandpa Simmons that Boyd is a deacon in the church and a member of the town planning board. She speaks in a soft voice and Ronnie must strain against the heavy pull of sleep to determine what she is saying. She mentions Boyd's plans to breed beef cattle. Ronnie is drowsing, almost asleep. He hears Grandpa Simmons caution her about the gossip that will be caused by having Boyd around too much and too soon after Hank's death. Grandpa Simmons' voice is not soft. It is harsh and admonishing. Ronnie opens his eyes quickly, and without focusing them, he determines that there is still daylight outside, although gray and overcast. He is overwhelmed by a comfortable limpness and by sleep.

Later he is aware for a moment of Virginia Jane, in her room alone, sobbing softly to herself. Another time he thinks that she is in his room, standing near his bed, but sleep draws him away and he is not sure that either one is real. Dreams and reality mix in Ronnie's interrupted sleep. He hears Grandpa Simmons shout:

"I gave you everything I had. The roof over my head."

The old man's anger bulges the veins in his neck. Ronnie can see this in the instant before he awakens and sits upright in his bed. He runs his fingers through his long brown hair. He swings his feet to the floor and sits on the edge of the bed rubbing his eyes, suspended between the shouting in his dreams and the shouting in the living room.

"Don't tell me to be quiet. This is my house." Grandpa Simmons' slurred words are coming from the living room. They are loud but remote, confusing to Ronnie. He slips on his shoes and walks to the windows. It is late afternoon and the room is dark. There is a faint pink glow on the horizon. The yard light is on and there are still several cars in the driveway. It is very still outside. The ground is hidden by the thick snow cover and there is no wind. He stands at the window for a silent moment, but the shouting voice erupts again:

"And don't you forget that this is my house. You're

the guest, not me. You never paid me a cent for this place. I always pay. I pay for everything. Every mistake you've ever made. I paid for that husband of yours who spent all his money on cars and motorcycles. And I'll pay for his funeral too."

Ronnie goes into the hallway, passes his parents' room and Bunnie's, and descends the winding front stairs. About halfway down he stops and leans over the bannister. Harry Fry is in the front hallway, leaning on the front door for support. He holds a beer can in his hand and is turned so he can view the commotion in the living room. He turns his red eyes on Ronnie, shrugs, and turns back to watch the fight in the living room. The little old man sways as he shouts, punctuating the air with his half-filled glass, splashing his drink on the carpet. His other hand grips his cane, but Ronnie is sure he will fall down.

"You always came back to this house. You left it when you were eighteen, and you came back to it with a baby. You came back to it again when you lost that farm in Iowa."

Ronnie advances, slowly. Drawn only by curiosity, he has no intention of interfering. He wants to leave soon with no complications. Virginia Jane is seated on the couch facing her father. She looks directly up at him and she seems about to cry. A floor lamp illuminates her face, and her mouth, which is distorted and turned down at the corners, silently forms the words "please," and "Father" over and over. Her hands nervously ball up and tug at a handkerchief in her lap. Other people in the room seem to be trying to ignore the tirade. Ronnie is near Harry Fry, and when he looks at his drunken cousin, Harry shrugs his shoulders again and blinks his red half-shut eyes. Now Boyd moves up beside Grandpa Simmons. He towers over the little man, whom he takes lightly by the elbow. Without looking at Boyd or even seeming to notice him, Grandpa Simmons angrily pulls his elbow away and shouts to his daughter:

"And you came back here when Hank moved out on you after he beat up that Timmons fellow you wanted to marry. I always took you in. I . . ."—he pounds his chest with the fist that holds the cane—"I gave you the best."

Virginia Jane suddenly drops her head and begins to sob. Ronnie, who is only six, cannot carry the heavy suitcase by himself, so he stops next to her on the snow-covered walk outside their apartment building and comforts her by putting his small arm around her waist. It is snowing and a light wind pushes the flakes diagonally across the wedge of light falling from the streetlamp. After a moment she composes herself, and together they pick up the suitcase—sharing the single handle—and walk to the running car in which Grandpa Simmons waits.

A gentle August breeze wafts over the month-old baby in the bassinet by the open window. Sunlight broken by the shifting leaves on the yard trees falls through the two western windows of the living room. The Sunday afternoon is relaxed and comfortable. Grandma Simmons has a white knit shawl draped over her shoulders as she sits at the piano in the living room. Virginia Jane, wearing a full and girlish lavender dress, stands beside the piano with her right arm resting on its top and her left hand holding a thin book of music in front of her. She is singing a song from Schumann's *Dichterliebe* cycle in a pleasant, occasionally strained soprano. She does not understand the German and she sings Heine's words to his beloved without emotion. The piano is much more than just an accompaniment in this song, and although she and her mother do not often work together, there is a proud smile on Grandpa Simmons' face as he sits on the couch next to Ronnie. Grandpa Simmons is wearing a white linen suit and a blue bow tie with tiny fleurs-de-lis of silver silk woven into it. In his enjoyment he leans forward with his palms resting on his knees. Ronnie is seated back against his cushion, and his legs with their Buster Brown shoes and white knee socks do not reach the floor. He is wearing a navy-blue suit with short pants and a blue tie with a single horizontal white stripe splitting its middle. His unruly brown hair has been wetted and plastered down with a part on the side. He changes position often, sitting up and slouching. Most of the time he looks out the open windows, never at his mother.

The song ends—the piano finishes slightly ahead of the voice—and Grandpa Simmons applauds and then stops abruptly when the baby begins to cry. Virginia Jane goes to the bassinet and lifts the infant out. The crying stops.

"You're going to spoil that girl," Grandpa Simmons says, standing up. "When you cried, we just let you lay. You pick the little girl up every time she whimpers."

He goes to the closet next to the mantel and takes from it two violin cases. When Virginia Jane sees the second violin case, she says:

"I don't feel like playing now, Daddy. I want to feed Bernice." She starts to undo the buttons at the top of her dress, beginning with the one at her neck.

"Then perhaps Ronnie can show us what he knows," Grandpa Simmons says, turning to the boy.

Ronnie lowers his eyes and looks at his white knee socks and heavy brown shoes. He does not accept or refuse the offer.

"Come on, now," Grandpa Simmons says to him, putting his mother's violin case in his lap. "Don't be bashful. We've all got to start somewhere."

Ronnie hesitates, wondering how he can get out of it. He looks to his mother who has seated herself across the room in an easy chair, but she has already exposed the right half of her large absorbent brassière. She is unfastening the hinged cup of the undergarment, and she urges Ronnie with her eyes to play for his grandfather. She pulls the cup down exposing her white distended breast with the slight trace of veins flowing down the vertical slope. The baby resting in the crook of her right arm begins a struggle to get at the milk, and Virginia Jane obliges by guiding the swollen brown nipple and aureole to its mouth. Ronnie opens the violin case and puts it on the couch beside himself. He stands up as the baby draws on the nipple greedily, its nose pressing tightly into the bulging soft flesh of the breast. By the time Ronnie has placed his music on the stand and lowered the stand to his height, the baby's eyes have started to close with drowsiness, although the suction of its mouth is just as firm as when it started to feed.

"Would you like me to play along?" Grandpa Simmons asks him.

"I couldn't keep up," Ronnie says. With no introduction, he launches into a labored and noisy version of one of his recently assigned exercises. The baby's eyes open wide on the frequent screeches, but it does not stop sucking. Grandpa Simmons is sitting on the couch in his upright position with his hands on his knees. Again he looks pleased, although this exercise is painfully played by Ronnie, who makes many mistakes, and repeats each of the notes he has botched. Virginia Jane slides her index finger into the baby's wet mouth as a replacement for the breast she now withdraws. A fine jet of milk sprays the baby's cheek, causing it to flinch. Virginia Jane wipes the baby's cheek with a tissue. Closing and fastening the cup of the brassière, she shifts the dress to cover it and expose its mate. Opening the other cup, she guides the baby to the fresh breast, and as it settles again to its meal, she relaxes and drops her head back on the easy chair to stare at the ceiling. Grandma Simmons, seated on the piano bench with her back to the piano, watches her with pride and perhaps a little maternal envy. Grandpa Simmons keeps his attention on Ronnie's playing, leaning forward to encourage him or to demonstrate a steady bowing technique on an imaginary violin. Ronnie watches the music nervously, but as his audience becomes more relaxed, he makes fewer mistakes. When he can, he glances at his mother and at the baby feeding at her white breast which is framed and strapped in by the whiter material of the nursing bra. Over these whites fall the dappled patterns of sunlight and shade, mixed and shifting in the breeze with hints of green from the elms and maples of the yard.

The leaves smash and fall apart as the fat angry motorcycles explode through the bushes at the top of the ridge. The first one through is Hank. Virginia Jane, who is swigging from a can of beer, cheers, spilling some of the beer. The hefty woman standing next to her, wearing tight bulging Levis, slaps her painfully on the back, spilling more beer, and shouts:

"Who else, honey? Who the hell else did you expect it to be?"

Virginia Jane barely hears her over the growl and scream of the pack of motorcycles bounding through the woods in close pursuit of Hank. Now the pack pours through the tattered and ever-widening hole in the brush at the top of the incline. The men in this pack are mud-splattered and intense. Their hostile machines speak for them as their booted feet kick at the ground and at the gearshifts in the guts of the machines. There is no mud on Hank's face, but he is as bent and intense as his pursuers, his elbows cocked up and out like stubby wings. The tight whine of his engine snaps into a growl as his foot quickly shifts to a higher gear, and he is still gaining speed when he hits a sharp dip in the path that shoots him and his machine off into the air as if his elbows had finally carried him aloft. The rear tire of the motorcycle touches ground first and then the front one settles and the machine seems ready to leap again. Hank has negotiated the jump, but suddenly his bike goes down, dropping sideways against the ground and spinning man and machine in a skidding circle along the rough woods path. Virginia Jane, clutching the beer can tightly and holding her black peaked captain's cap with her other hand, is running toward him almost as soon as he drops. Ronnie runs after her, releasing his grip on his small sister's hand. When Bunnie sees that she has been abandoned, she begins to cry, but does not move from the spot on which she stands. Two more motorcycles drop to the ground as the pursuing riders take the jump and try to avoid Hank. Hank is up almost immediately, sprinting down the path, pushing his stalled and mud-caked motorcycle. After a short dash, he leaps on the heavy machine, but it fails to catch, and he slips off quickly and continues his straining sprint down the path. He bounces onto the saddle of the machine three more times before giving up on it. As Virginia Jane and Ronnie reach him, they can hear him shout: "Well, fuck you then" to the bike which he pushes angrily off the path and down on its side. He walks away from it tugging his helmet gingerly over the spot on his cheek where a trickle of blood is mixing with the mud. When he sees Virginia Jane he begins to laugh and hands her the helmet to hold. His hair is curled and matted with sweat, and his Levis are ripped open to expose his bleeding knee. He takes the can she holds and drains off the beer without lowering his head. There is a small twig embedded in the muddy blood of the hand that holds the can. The little finger is bent sharply over the back of his hand and wobbles loosely while Hank drinks the beer. He tosses the empty can into the woods, ruffles Ronnie's hair with his good hand and throws his muddy arm around Virginia Jane's neck.

"You shouldn't ride those fucking things when you're drunk," he says. "Dangerous business." He laughs again, and then repeats his statement to one of the men who is painfully getting to his feet near his own spilled bike. The three of them walk back to Bunnie who is crying in the hefty woman's arms. By the time they reach her, they can hear the roar of the first motorcycles coming up the incline for the second lap of the race. As the leader shoots through the hole in the brush, Hank curses him and his own misfortune.

"I could've stopped for a nap and still won that scramble," he tells Virginia Jane. She has seen his broken finger and tries to examine it but he keeps it away from her, and tells her to wait until after the race. He opens another can of beer. There are no more mishaps in the race, and the motorcycles do not change positions again. The man who took the lead after Hank's spill wins the race. The riders, mud-splattered in leather and heavy denim and sweating in the chill spring air, gather around Hank to look at his finger and the cuts on his face. They tease him about plowing up the woods path, and they tell him he ought to stick to racing cars. Several of them help him get his motorcycle started again. Virginia Jane asks him to go to a doctor and get the finger set, but he says it can wait until he cleans and checks out his bike. She insists that he go right now, and she keeps after him while he works on the motorcycle. When he finally blows up, it is the first time since his return that Ronnie has heard him mention his two-year absence. He threatens to go away again, saying he is fed up with living on someone else's farm. He boasts that his income as a mechanic is the only thing that keeps the farm going anyway.

The people at this picnic and motorcycle scramble are mostly his friends, and Virginia Jane is embarrassed by his shouting. Another race is beginning, however, and most of the attention is devoted to the starting line where ten motorcycles snarl and spit beneath their hunched-up masters. As the flag drops and the ten roar down the hill and disappear into the woods, the temptation is too much for Hank. He fires his bike with one stomp of his heavy boot and leaps on. "I'm going to a doctor on this," he tells her. "You drive the car to the farm. I'll meet you there."

Ronnie and his baby sister sleep in the back seat of the car on the ride home. Ronnie awakens when the car stops at the side of a road near the farm. Virginia Jane is pulling a fluffy white sweater on over the tight black turtleneck jersey she has worn all day. In his half-sleep Ronnie is pleased that his mother is so pretty and young. He watches her lean over to stuff the peaked cap into the glove compartment. When he sees that she is about to put two sticks of chewing gum into her mouth, he asks her for one. She gives it to him and he climbs into the front seat for the remainder of the drive home. When they reach the farm, Hank is already there, seated at the kitchen table giving Grandpa Simmons an animated account of the races as if they are fast friends. Three fingers peek out of the fresh white cast that covers Hank's left hand and wrist.

Boyd again takes Grandpa Simmons by the arm. The old man is still tottering in front of his daughter. This time he does not pull away from Boyd, but turns to the tall cowboy searching for a sympathetic ear.

"Hank killed her mother." Tears replace the anger. Boyd nods sympathetically. Ronnie turns and starts back up the stairs. "He was too rough for her. He frightened her. He drove me right out of my own house." Down the length of the hall Ronnie can still hear him. "We're tasteful people here. Gentle people with good breeding. He filled our gardens with engines and junk cars and grease. We never . . ." Ronnie slams the door to his room and stops the lamentation. He slides the suitcase out from under the bed, opens it on the floor and checks its contents. Standing up, he slips his tie off and hurriedly removes his suitcoat. He pushes these into the suitcase without folding them properly and then forces the top down with his knee and closes the snaps again. From his dresser he takes a sweater and pulls it on over his white dress shirt. He then goes to his closet, and as he bends over to pick up his gym bag which is filled with his boxing equipment—shoes, trunks, protector, socks, tape—the door to his room opens and Boyd and Virginia Jane lead a very white-faced Grandpa Simmons to Ronnie's bed. The old man is breathing hard, and the three of them must step over the suitcase before Grandpa Simmons can lie down on the bed. Virginia Jane begins to remove the old man's shoes and Boyd loosens his tie.

"Do you think he'll be sick again?" Boyd asks her.

"No," she answers. "He should go to sleep." She takes his wire-rimmed glasses off and puts them on the table beside the bed.

"No need to sleep," Grandpa Simmons says, but his eyes are already closing.

Virginia Jane sees Ronnie for the first time when he shuts the closet door.

"What's in this suitcase?" she demands.

"My stuff," Ronnie tells her flatly.

"Where are you going with it?"

"Out of here." Ronnie crosses the room with his gym bag in his hand. As he bends to pick up the suitcase, Virginia Jane puts her foot on it and says:

"Not tonight, you're not." She shifts her weight to the foot, and Ronnie must tug at the suitcase to get it loose. She stumbles against Boyd when Ronnie jerks it free, and the big man says: "Watch it, boy," flexing an angry fist at Ronnie. Ronnie, with a bag in each hand, heads for the door, but Boyd dashes ahead of him and blocks him off.

"Your mother doesn't want you to go," he warns Ronnie.

As Ronnie and Boyd confront each other at the door, Grandpa Simmons suddenly shouts:

"Let him go. Let him go." He does not sit up, but instead yells his words at the ceiling from his prone position. "He's just like his father anyway, the sullen bastard. Go on, let him go. This house is better without him. I might even come back if he's not around."

Boyd backs through the door and Ronnie darts past him. Boyd is still blocking the back stairs, so Ronnie hurries quickly down the hall to the front of the house. Boyd and Virginia Jane follow him, leaving Grandpa Simmons behind. Ronnie can hear him shouting as he descends the front steps. "He's a killer, that boy. Ask him how many women and children he killed over in the jungles. He doesn't like the good gentle things in life. He's not bred well."

Virginia Jane grabs Ronnie's arm halfway down the steps, and to avoid an accident, he stops, drops his gym bag and tries to pry her hand loose.

"I need you here. Don't you see that?" She descends two more steps so she can look at his face. "I loved your father, and now I need you more than ever." Ronnie looks from her to Boyd who is standing beside him. Boyd's face is bland and indicates nothing. "Don't leave Bernice and me alone." Almost on cue, Bunnie appears in the dining-room doorway and looks up at the scene on the steps. Harry Fry is still propped drunkenly against the front door. Ronnie picks up the gym bag and slowly makes his way down the steps, tugging along Virginia Jane who will not release her grip. "Please, Ronnie, don't leave me alone." There is desperation in her voice and for a moment Ronnie hesitates. At the bottom of the steps, she releases her grip when Harry Fry throws his arm around Ronnie's shoulders. Beer from his can splashes on Ronnie's sweater.

"Hey, Ron," he breathes, oblivious to the argument and to Boyd and Virginia Jane standing tensely at the foot of the steps. "Hey Ron hey. Remember that time on my dad's boat when Alton Stevens cut the end off Hank's thumb in the drag winch." Harry Fry's frazzled young wife comes from the living room and begins to tug at her husband's sleeve. Her eyes are surrounded by dark circles and she seems crushed with exhaustion. "Please, honey," she says in a soft voice which Harry Fry doesn't hear.

" 'Jesus Christ, Alton,' Hank says to him. 'You've cut off my fuckin' thumb.' Then he finds the tip and puts it on a hook and runs it out, and damned if we didn't catch a mackerel with it. You got sick when you saw the squirting stump. You was about eleven or twelve. Boy, they was some drunk that Sunday. I must have been about sixteen, and I had to take the boat in for them. Caught a whole bushel of mackerel too."

"Hold the door," Ronnie tells him suddenly.

A look of confusion crosses Harry Fry's face, and his wife jerks the door open. Ronnie slips out quickly.

"What about the gas station?" Boyd yells after him.

Ronnie sprints for his car carrying the bags, but Virginia Jane comes right after him, hurrying over the snow in her black dress. She catches him at the car.

"Ronnie, please," she says, trying to catch her breath. "If you leave, the pressure on me will be unbearable." She nods toward the towering figure of Boyd now framed by the light of the open doorway. When Ronnie looks at him, he sees that Harry Fry and his wife are peering around Boyd's shoulders. Bunnie is watching through the dining-room window and several of the remaining guests have come to the living-room windows to watch. Ronnie puts the bags in the back seat of the car and avoids looking at his mother who is twisting her handkerchief nervously in her fingers. "Please," she says again, as her breathing becomes more regular. "I think your grandfather wants to move back here again. He can't stand Florida, and I can't tell him no. I need time. Just stay until I can come to the proper decision."

Ronnie shakes his head no and slips into the car. Boyd is approaching from the porch. Harry Fry now stands weaving in the doorway, scratching his head and peering toward the car.

Boyd's hand is out as he approaches, but Ronnie slams the car door. "No hard feelings, boy," he says. "It's no good to leave with hard feelings. Here's your pay."

Ronnie sees that he is offering four ten dollar bills toward him, and reluctantly he rolls down the window and accepts them. He must accept Boyd's handshake first, and when he takes the money he drops it on the seat beside him and starts the car without rolling the window up again.

"Good luck tonight, boy," Boyd says. His gestures are fatherly and nervous. "I hope you knock 'em dead. I think I'm going to drive in and see the fight."

Virginia Jane says something but Ronnie is already pumping the gas pedal, and the rumble and crack of his muffler drowns out her words. He roars away from them, skidding out onto the main road toward the pink glow that sits at the bottom of the iron gray sky.

# IV

Boyd waves encouragement to Ronnie from his seat three rows back from ringside in the dark smoky auditorium. Ronnie eyes him without nodding and bends over the bucket at the foot of his stool and spits out the water he has been swishing around in his mouth. He expects to see a stain of red in the water just as he had expected to see the same stain on his mouthpiece when he spit it into the outstretched hand of the club manager at the end of the round. But there is none, even though his mouth hurts like hell. His opponent, the pretty boy named Maurie Jacobs, clipped him good at the end of the round; nothing damaging except Ronnie thinks he is cut inside his mouth somewhere, although there is no blood as yet. The fighters have spent the first two rounds cautiously feeling each other out and attacking and retreating. Ronnie calculates that the rounds were scored evenly, but the manager, the little man whom most of the local fighters pay to come to the corner with them since a second is required and who seldom has more to tell you than you already know, tells him that Jacobs has the edge and that Ronnie will have to go on the offensive if he wants to get some points. But Jacobs doesn't like to get hit. He has been inviting Ronnie to chase him, and Ronnie knows from seeing him previously that Jacobs' fight is to counterpunch, and that he is quick and strong and will make Ronnie look silly if he does move after him. Ronnie spots Gus, the promoter, in his seat just before the bell rings, and Gus mouths the warning he delivered earlier in his dressing room: "Let's see a fight." The bell rings and Ronnie moves out to meet Jacobs, who begins to circle even as he moves out of his corner. Jacobs is taller than Ronnie and leaner. His black hair is long and slicked back on the sides like Ronnie's. As yet, very little of it is out of place, although it is matted and dripping with perspiration where it falls in a straight line across his neck. Jacobs is wearing shiny black trunks with a white stripe and Ronnie wears the opposite, white with a black stripe. They both wear high black boxing shoes. Their slim, hard-muscled bodies are winter pale in the glare of the ring lights as they cautiously circle. The referee, a squat rough-looking man wearing a white shirt open at the collar, follows in the same circle, watching them carefully. They draw closer to each other, and when they meet, there is an exchange of lefts and they move apart. Ronnie can hear some derisive comments from the crowd. Jacobs does not seem to hear them, but instead watches Ronnie with cold, professional concentration. Ronnie wants to give the crowd a fight, but he is still not sure how far he can go. More than a beating, he's afraid he will tire too early, look bad and lose the chance for another hundred-dollar fight. He feels fine now after two rounds, just getting warm. He has never tired excessively in a four-round bout, except for arm weariness if it turned into a slugging match. But if he moves in, forcing the fight, Jacobs will punch him silly, while he wastes his energy chasing the pretty boy. The two fighters throw some more easy lefts, and this time there are boos from the crowd when they back off. Ronnie moves in again suddenly and punches two hard left hooks on the side of Jacobs' head. Jacobs is expecting the move and digs a crushing left of his own into Ronnie's stomach. It lands and sinks painfully, and Ronnie turns and traps the left under his arm, but instead of clinching, he brings up two inside swats to Jacobs' head and dances back. The crowd likes it and there are some shouts and mild applause. Jacobs has taken Ronnie's punches so he could throw the hurting left. He is after Ronnie's body, thinking that Ronnie is a local fighter with a hard head and only fair, if not poor, conditioning—which is mostly true. But something else has also clicked in Ronnie's head. Jacobs tried the same exchange earlier in the fight but Ronnie had backed off and the pretty boy had been unable to use it. Perhaps he has a one-track mind. Thinks up something and then has to use it, over and over again. Ronnie must take advantage of it. Move quickly, kill quickly. The crowd begins to grumble again, and Ronnie throws a long right, or rather fakes it, stops it three-quarters of the way through and dances back as Jacobs slides right and coils his own right arm for two or three savage body shots, his left already moving back for the head try. Now, to test the counterpuncher's imagination, Ronnie throws the long right again, almost instantly after the other one.

But he goes through with it this time, shifting slightly to his own right. And again Jacobs' savage short rights come into Ronnie's stomach but grazing the left side, not where they are supposed to be. Ronnie is zigging and Jacobs is zagging, and while those body punches are being thrown, Ronnie snaps Jacobs' head with a hard left hook. Jacobs never gets to throw his left as Ronnie's right crosses it and catches square the extended jaw. Jacobs goes down, not crumpled but stiff—boom—on the hard canvas. Crumples into the snow, and Hank drops the board and stands over him. Ronnie does not know Jacobs is down, or rather he cannot conceive that the combination has worked so well, so early. So lucky? He stands over him, puffing slightly, wanting to swing his fists which are now tucked up at his sides. The referee pushes him back and Ronnie trots to the far corner. The noise of the crowd explodes into his ears. The people are on their feet roaring, beating each other. What is the matter with Jacobs? The pretty boy lies there, his eyes open, his head held up about two inches off the canvas, his legs so stiff the muscles in his thighs bulge. Cold-cocked. Ronnie is frightened; he rolls up the window so Hank will not hear him cry. Hank stumbles to the steps of the porch. Jacobs is looking directly at Ronnie, but Ronnie knows he cannot see him. Ronnie has hurt him. How badly? He waits, trembling inside, for the count to reach ten. He does not want Jacobs to get up; does not want to do any more of this tonight. But he wants Jacobs to get up, not to be badly hurt, to dance and jab and hit him and be hit and to be knocked out; but to crumple, to stumble around trying to get up and stand and waver and have the referee stop it and declare Ronnie the winner and have Jacobs slouch over—slightly groggy—and congratulate him. Not lie there stiff and look at him, his head held tight, two inches off the canvas. Ronnie drops to a crouch and then crawls forward to the edge of the loft. Hank is sprawled on the floor beside the pink coupé, blood running swiftly from his nose and mouth. The wind flaps the collar of his red wool jacket against his jaw. The referee is holding Ronnie's hand aloft, and Ronnie is barely aware of this. He is watching Jacobs' manager and trainer bolt into the ring and push ammonia-soaked cotton under the prone fighter's nose. Jacobs bats at the harsh smell once and then relaxes, collapses, and still Ronnie stands in the corner staring, trembling inside. The house lights go on. Ronnie is aware of small boys in the ring, pushing at him, tugging at his trunks; and of two cops peeling them away from him. The club manager puts Ronnie's robe over his shoulders and shakes his glove and then says: "Go over and see him, Ronnie," and Ronnie starts across the ring. He hears the scream of the crowd, and his knees bubble and shake. He kneels beside Jacobs. His head is pressed against the chest and his hands hold the wrist tightly. Wind flaps Hank's collar. Jacobs' eyes are closed, and Ronnie asks the fat man kneeling next to him if he will be O.K. Just then Jacobs' eyelids flutter and the man pushes the ammonia cotton in again and Jacobs pulls his head away and opens his eyes wide—the same look as when he was stiff—and closes them again. His body starts to move and Ronnie and the two men pick him up and drag him to his corner where they hold him slumped on his stool. "He'll be O.K., kid," the fat man says to Ronnie, and Ronnie walks back across the ring and stands in his corner while the club manager unties his gloves. When the gloves are off, he sees them helping Jacobs down the ring steps, and he waits until the stumbling fighter is halfway back through the crowd toward the downstairs locker rooms before he ducks through the ropes himself, holding them apart with his taped hands while the manager follows carrying his gloves. He is watching Jacobs intently and he is startled by Boyd, who is waiting for him at the bottom of the steps.

"Nice fight, son. Nice fight," the big man says, pumping his hand.

Behind Boyd is Gus, the promoter. He reaches forward and takes the hand away from Boyd and says: "Now that's what they come to see, kid. Exactly what they come to see. You make sure you get that check at the box office tonight. And why don't you come and see me tomorrow?"

"I'll make sure he does," Boyd tells the squat little man.

Ronnie walks absently away from them and pushes his way down the aisle. People tug at him and slap his back and touch him as he walks. His robe keeps slipping from his shoulders and he balls it up and carries it in his arms. As he walks, he watches Jacobs with his trainer and his manager trying to negotiate the steps down to the locker rooms at the back of the auditorium. When Ronnie reaches the steps, Jack Forgione, a heavyweight with whom Ronnie sometimes trains, is standing there in his robe and trunks, ready for the semifinal, leaning against the concrete-block wall, waiting for Ronnie to complete his exit, not wanting to upstage him, waiting for the noisy buzz from the crowd to calm down. He puts his arm around Ronnie's neck and walks down three steps and says: "What was that bag of bones that just went past me? Was it that nice kid from New Jersey who comes up here to Maine to fight us hicks?" Forgione is tall with bulging chunky muscles. He has a very low forehead separating his thick, close-cropped black hair and his bushy eyebrows. The forehead, like the nape of his squat neck, is divided into three ridges. Like Ronnie, one of his eyebrows is split by a thin scar of white flesh. Ronnie looks at him, puzzled, but Forgione's wide grin above his massive jaw is irresistible and Ronnie grins back at him. Forgione squeezes Ronnie's sweating neck and says: "He's O.K., Ron. Don't worry about him. You won." And Ronnie *has* won. He hurries down the steps, still carrying his robe under his arm, trailed by the manager who carries his gloves.

"Did you see the look on his face?" Ronnie asks, sitting on the bench in front of his locker while the manager cuts the tape from his hands. "He was out cold. And surprised too." The manager nods and laughs with Ronnie. He is a small man with a thin black mustache, and he wears a white tee shirt and a beige cardigan sweater with cotton swabs in the pockets. He has no more fighters tonight. Forgione in the semifinal is the last local boy and he has his own manager. The fighters in the final are professionals from Boston and Providence.

"Gus'll get you a good fight for that one," he tells Ronnie. "You keep that up and I wouldn't be surprised if somebody who knew something about fighting took you under his wing."

"I don't need a permanent manager," Ronnie tells him. "You're good enough for me."

"I mean somebody big. Somebody like Cus D'Amato. I hear he's looking for somebody your weight."

"Who, me? What would somebody that big want with me?"

"Why not?" He snips the last of the tape. "How old are you?"

"Twenty-one."

"You got your service over?"

"Discharged six months ago."

"He could build you into something."

Ronnie laughs at him and pushes him playfully away. He steps out of his trunks and protector and walks to the shower. Ronnie hurries so he can go back upstairs to watch the next fight, and to let the crowd see him in his street clothes and gym bag—the killer.

But first he walks down the hall to the other locker room to check on Jacobs. He finds the fighter still in his trunks lying face up on the rubdown table. The room is heavy with smells of ammonia and vomit. Jacobs' hands are still taped and his arm is thrown across his eyes against the glare of the overhead bulb. His trainer stands at the far end of the table untying Jacobs' ring shoes. Ronnie is not sure Jacobs is conscious, but he asks: "How you feeling?"

"Hungover," Jacobs answers, taking his arm away and eyeing Ronnie without raising his head.

"Nice fight," Ronnie tells him.

"Yeh, nice fight yourself." Jacobs speaks softly as if he is afraid of jarring something. His face is gray. A bucket is beside the table.

Outside in the echoing concrete hallway Ronnie asks the manager about Jacobs' condition. The fat man says he probably has a concussion, and they'll ride over to the hospital when they get him dressed. The ring doctor told them he should spend the night there. Ronnie scribbles his home telephone number on a piece of paper and tells the man to call him later when they have more information. Then he remembers he doesn't live there anymore.

As he starts up the steel steps to the auditorium, the man, still standing by the door, holding the piece of paper, says:

"He's gonna fight you again, kid. Maybe next time you won't be so lucky."

Ronnie turns and smiles at him, a wide smile that shows his missing tooth. "You think he'll want to?" Ronnie can hear Jacobs vomiting behind the door.

"He'll want to," the man says.

"See Gus then," Ronnie tells him. "I don't make no fights." His double negative is out of character and mocks the gangster-Jersey accent of the fat man. Ronnie turns and runs up the steps two at a time, his gym bag slapping at his leg.

Boyd is waiting for him at the top of the steps. He is talking to the policeman who has kept him from going down into the locker-room area. The policeman looks to Ronnie for reassurance, but when he sees that Ronnie knows Boyd, he apologizes. Boyd commends him for doing his job. Behind Boyd and the policeman, Ronnie can see the smoky bright light of the ring over the silhouetted heads of the darkened crowd. Forgione in his purple trunks is circling the ring, stalking carefully around a powerful-looking Negro wearing white trunks. The Negro turns with Forgione but does not move from the center of the ring. Forgione dances in, and they exchange heavy punches and then separate. The crowd is murmuring with little reaction, and Ronnie guesses the fight has just begun. He thinks of slipping past Boyd to find a seat to hide in. But the auditorium is small and Boyd will seek him out.

"I have your seat for you, Ron," Boyd says, turning to him.

"O.K." Ronnie follows Boyd down the aisle, but his eyes are on the fight, which is partly blocked off from him by the tall man's cowboy hat.

"That was quite a fight, son," the man next to Boyd leans over to tell him after they are seated. It is between rounds, and Forgione is relaxing in his corner while his manager explains something to him. "Mr. Boyd here tells me you're Hank Mandeville's boy," the man continues.

"What's that?" Ronnie asks, turning to him.

"Hank Mandeville. You're his boy," the man repeats.

"Yes," Ronnie says.

"I saw him race many a time," the man says. A buzzer sounds, warning the fighters that there are ten seconds remaining until the start of round two. "I think he was one of the finest drivers in New England."

"He was," Ronnie answers, turning to watch Forgione again.

"I'm sorry to hear about him passing away."

"Thank you," Ronnie tells the man, looking at him quickly and then turning his attention back to the ring. The bell rings and Forgione rushes across the ring to meet the Negro fighter, who stands up slowly from his stool.

"Our people were Scottish," the man continues.

"What?" Ronnie asks him without looking at him.

"Scots. They settled first in Nova Scotia."

The Negro suddenly lashes out with a swift combination of punches that surprises Forgione and drives him back across the ring and against the ropes. The crowd explodes into a collective roar and leaps to its feet.

Ronnie is up shouting to Forgione to clinch. The man beside Boyd also stands and says:

"I don't recall ever hearing the name Mandeville in these parts. What is it? French?"

Forgione clinches safely and the referee separates the two fighters. He does not seem to be hurt.

The crowd sits down, and Ronnie asks the man to repeat what he said.

"What's Mandeville? French?" the man asks.

"My dad is from Iowa," Ronnie tells him.

The crowd roars and leaps again, and Ronnie looks into the ring to see the Negro on his back, his legs askew above him. He rolls quickly to his feet, and Ronnie can see Forgione laughing at him. The Negro smiles too as the referee wipes the gloves on his white shirt. The fighters come back together, touch gloves and then circle, jabbing lightly with their left hands.

"What part of Iowa?" the man asks.

The man is still standing, and Ronnie draws a knee up quickly into his groin. The man doubles over in pain, and Ronnie twines his hands together and strikes down like an ax on the man's nape.

"Hey, c'mon. Let's watch the fight," Ronnie tells him and smiles, wiping his lips with the back of his hand.

"Sure. Sure. O.K.," the man says, sitting back in his seat and folding his arms across his chest. Ronnie watches him for a moment curiously, but the man is now looking intently into the ring.

The remainder of the round is uneventful, and when it is over, a number of Ronnie's friends—most of them connected one way or another with fighting—come to his seat to congratulate him. Some of them tease him and make a show of feeling his muscles, and others imitate Jacobs, falling back on their friends in a mock knockout. People continue to seek him out between rounds. Some of them are strangers whom Ronnie greets politely. Two small boys ask him for his autograph, and although he is surprised by the request, he casually obliges them. Several of the boxers have girls with them, and Ronnie's desire for a girl competes with the growing discomfort in his empty stomach.

The fight is a slugging match, but neither Forgione nor the Negro is knocked down again. Both have swollen eyes when the six rounds are over and both are battered and exhausted. The crowd applauds for them when the final bell sounds, and as they stand in the center of the ring arm in arm congratulating each other, Boyd, who has not spoken since the fight started, leans toward Ronnie and says:

"I think the nigger won it. What do you think?"

"Let's wait and see," Ronnie tells him. He is watching the referee collect scoring cards from the judges.

"What makes you think Forgione has it?" Boyd asks.

"I didn't say he did."

"Who do you pick then? The nigger?"

"I don't pick anybody. The fight was even. Forgione is the local boy. Everybody likes him and he has to fight here again. Gus needs all the help he can get with the local favorites." Ronnie looks toward the promoter's seat, but it is empty.

"I don't think the judges would do anything that isn't fair."

Ronnie doesn't answer him. Forgione is leaning on the ropes in his corner wearing a purple silk bathrobe and a towel draped over his sweaty head. He is beckoning to Ronnie. Ronnie goes out of his row past Boyd and up the steps to his friend. Forgione is still slightly out of breath. With the corner of the towel he wipes at the sweat dripping from his nose and lips.

"If I win this fight," he tells Ronnie confidentially, "you and me are going to get so fucking drunk we'll have to hold each other up."

Forgione's swollen eye looks painful, and he leans heavily on the ropes beside Ronnie. The referee hands the score cards to the announcer sitting at ringside in front of his microphone, Ronnie leans on the ropes and both fighters become silent, as does the crowd. In the opposite corner, the Negro does an unenthusiastic dance to keep warm while his handlers watch the announcer. The first judge awards the fight to Forgione, and the sweating fighter grunts his approval but does not look up. The Negro stops dancing and his eyes fall on the announcer. The second judge scores the fight evenly, and Forgione says to Ronnie without looking up:

"It's gonna be a fucking draw, and if it is, we'll really get drunk."

The big fighter leaps high in the air and comes down with his arms around his manager when the referee's score is read giving the decision to him. Forgione raises both his gloved hands in the air and the referee helps to hold the left one aloft to signify that he is the winner. The Negro comes over to congratulate him, and Ronnie hears him say:

"Come down to Worcester, man. We'll see who wins down there."

"Speak to the man here," Forgione says, nodding his head to indicate his manager. He turns away, and the sweating black fighter walks back to his corner, slips through the ropes and is gone.

"Come on downstairs," Forgione says to Ronnie as he ducks through the ropes and descends the three steps to the floor of the auditorium.

"I want to get some hot dogs," Ronnie tells him. "Come up and sit with me for the final." He points to the general area of his seat.

"Is there room?" Forgione asks.

"We'll make room," Ronnie says, and Forgione leaves, hurrying down the aisle through the handshakes and touches of the crowd.

Ronnie must walk past Boyd to get to the refreshment stand, and when he reaches him, he asks the big man if he wants anything brought back.

"Wait, I'll go along," Boyd answers.

There is already a crowd around the refreshment counters, and while Ronnie is waiting to get at the hot-dog section, Boyd says:

"I see you already got your hotel room."

"What hotel room?" Ronnie counters.

They are jammed and jostled by the hungry crowd, and

an occasional well-wisher shakes Ronnie's hand or points him out to a friend.

"The one you were going to get when you left home," Boyd tells him.

"I . . . ah . . . didn't get it yet." Ronnie is not speaking directly to Boyd, but instead is turned away stretching his neck to watch over the heads of the crowd for Forgione.

"Oh, I thought that's where you left your suitcase," Boyd says.

"It's in the trunk of the car." Ronnie levels a look at Boyd who is nervously feeling for information.

"Is there a girl, Ron? Is that where the suitcase is? Just between you and me. Man to man."

A space opens in front of Ronnie and he moves forward a step. "Man to man, I wish there was," he laughs. "I haven't had a piece of ass since I got back in the States."

"Your mother thinks that's why you want to leave," Boyd says, moving up beside him.

"What do you think?" Ronnie asks, turning on him again.

"I think you're restless, boy. It's natural. What do you think I'm doing here instead of Wyoming? I was restless. Why, when I got back to the States in 1946, I spent an entire summer following the wheat harvest north across the plains. Just a plain old itinerant, me and a buddy of mine that was from New York City that I met in Japan. We had an old car, a Model A with a crank on it that we slept in when we weren't sleeping in the fields or in a barn. We worked from sunup to sundown. And we'd talk at night or in the car when we were driving to the next job. That was the best summer of my life." Boyd looks away thoughtfully. The crowd opens in front of him and he moves up to the counter.

"That's about it," Ronnie says. "I'm just restless."

"I know, boy," Boyd tells him. "It's nothing new." He has turned his back to the counter, while Ronnie gestures to the frantic, sweating hot-dog man. "It's just that you're doing it at the wrong time."

Ronnie does not answer him, but continues to wave his index finger over Boyd's head at the man behind the counter.

"Your mother needs the support now. She needs a man in the house."

Ronnie stops waving his finger—although he leaves it in the air—and asks: "What about you? You were doing more around that house than Hank was. I don't guess you're going to stop now."

"Your mother and I have agreed not to make any plans for six months."

"So you need me around to chaperone."

"That's not the point at all."

"What is the point? What are you doing here?"

"I promised her I'd bring you back."

The hot-dog man finally responds to Ronnie's upraised finger.

"What do you want?" Boyd asks, withdrawing his wallet.

"I'll get it," Ronnie tells him.

"Never mind," Boyd insists. "It's on me."

"Four," Ronnie tells the hot-dog man. "With mustard and onions. And a Coke."

Boyd, who gets nothing for himself, carries three of the hot dogs and the Coke as they work their way back through the crowd. When they are crossing the open area between the crush of people at the refreshment stand and the seats, Boyd stops Ronnie and says:

"I don't know how to tell you this. It's very confidential, and I hope that anything I say to you won't be repeated."

Ronnie stuffs the second half of his hot dog into his

mouth. When Boyd pauses, Ronnie takes another hot dog and the Coke from his hands. He sips from the Coke while he chews and then replaces the cup in Boyd's outstretched hand. Boyd does not seem to notice the transaction. He is looking earnestly into Ronnie's eyes.

"Boy," he says. "My plans for you include even more than I could tell you this morning." He removes his tan hat and looks around cautiously. Ronnie watches his second hot dog from which he has just taken a bite. Boyd leans down toward him and in a secretive voice says:

"Our planning board is in the midst of working with a corporation that wants to put a huge shopping center out on the Barrow Point Road. This is secret, mind you, and is not to be repeated." Ronnie bites into the hot dog again although he has not altogether swallowed the previous mouthful. "This looks like it's going through now, and since we started working with these people, I've been able to acquire a good chunk of property out there. No prime sites, of course. They won't have to buy from me to build the place because I wouldn't use my position for anything as illegal as that. What I've got is some of the surrounding property, all with frontage on the highway. Once that shopping center is up, it'll make the best darn site for a gas station in the state."

Boyd pauses to give Ronnie a chance to comment. Ronnie stuffs the remainder of the hot dog in his mouth, and takes the Coke and another hot dog from Boyd.

"And that's not all," Boyd continues. He strides up the steps of the front porch without noticing Hank and Ronnie bent over the fender of the 1949 Ford Ronnie has just purchased. Hank is showing Ronnie how to replace the carburetor they have cleaned.

"Isn't that the guy who owns the gas station in town near the bridge?" Ronnie asks.

"That's him," Hank says. He does not look up from his

work. It is an early May Sunday, and the sound of a tractor plowing a field nearby drifts to them now and then on the sweet morning air.

"Does he want you?" Ronnie, like Hank, remains bent into the engine compartment of the car while he talks.

"He wants your mother," Hank tells him. "He's gonna take her to church."

"What for?"

"She wants to go."

"Why him?"

"Well"—the man with the beige cowboy hat has gone into the house, and Hank stands up beside the car—"you see, they're having a spirit drive, and Mr. Boyd is on the round-up committee. He even asked me if I'd come." Father and son smile at each other. "Hell, can you see the steeple fall off that church if I walked inside?" They laugh.

The front door opens and Virginia Jane and Boyd come out into the cool sunshine on the front porch. Bunnie trails them and shuts the door behind herself.

"Morning, Mr. Boyd," Hank says. Ronnie stands up beside him and gawks at the big man descending the steps beside his mother.

"Morning, Mr. Mandeville. Sure you won't change your mind?"

"Not this morning, Mr. Boyd."

"How about you, boy?"

Ronnie continues to gawk until Hank nudges him. Then he says:

"No, sir. I just bought this Ford here, and we're fixing it up."

"Perhaps some other morning then," Boyd says and escorts the woman and the child to his station wagon. Ronnie and Hank bend to their work, and when the station wagon is gone, Ronnie asks:

"Is he a cowboy or something?"

"He was," Hank says. He turns his head to smile conspiratorially at his son. "He used to ride in rodeos. Pretty big name too, if you can believe the stories you hear."

Boyd may be a real cowboy, but Ronnie knows that to Hank he is just a dude.

They replace the carburetor and connect it to the fuel line, and Ronnie starts the car's engine. Hank makes a few minor adjustments, and then they let the car stand with the engine running until it warms. They walk to the porch steps and sit in the sun. Hank offers Ronnie a cigarette from the wrinkled pack in his shirt pocket and lights it for him, cupping his grease-stained hands around the match to protect it from the soft May breeze that smells of raw earth and spring buds. They smoke together silently until Hank says:

"Comes originally from Wyoming."

"What?" Ronnie asks. He has been thinking about the car, about driving to the beach in it, driving a certain girl to the beach in it.

"That guy Boyd."

"Oh, him. Wyoming? What's he doing down here?"

"Wanted to settle, I guess. Story goes he walked off the rodeo in New York City five years ago and came to Maine. I hear he used to be a wild man too. But he's all morally *ree*-tributed now. He's a deacon in the Congregational Church and on the goddamn school committee even though he's a bachelor."

They finish their cigarettes and flick them out onto the bare hard earth of the yard. Hank begins to make mysterious adjustments in the newly cleaned carburetor with a screwdriver. First he adjusts the throttle and then he blends the air and fuel mixture until the engine is running with a smooth rich hum. Ronnie watches him carefully.

"Now," Hank says as he replaces the awkward-looking

air filter on the carburetor, "get a socket wrench and pull those spark plugs." Ronnie is amazed at how surely and quickly Hank works. Things seem to get done almost magically.

As Ronnie reaches for a wrench in the large metal tool box that sits on the gravel at the front of the car, Hank says: "Don't you think you'd better shut the engine off?"

"Oh, yes," Ronnie says, embarrassed.

"And wipe your hands before you touch my tools. You get so much grease on them, it takes me three passes just to pick one up."

Ronnie laughs and Hank hands him the rag, filthy with grease, from his back pocket.

As Ronnie unscrews each spark plug from its hole near the base of the engine, Hank stands behind him and watches over his shoulder. Ronnie is struggling with a particularly tight plug when Hank says:

"I hear he killed a man once."

Ronnie does not look up. He thinks of asking who or what, but he knows the answers to those questions, so he says nothing as he continues to struggle with the plug. He is eighteen, and it is four years since his visit with Carl Timmons' parents. It is the closest he ever comes to asking Hank about Timmons. The urge wells up in him, but Hank continues to talk.

"Killed another rodeo guy. But you can't believe everything you hear."

Ronnie looks down at the car's engine.

"He doesn't drink or cuss or fight anymore," Hank adds.

The plug breaks loose, and with a grunt, Ronnie begins to unscrew it.

"You'll be managing that one too someday," Boyd says. "We'll probably put in a body shop and get a full-time mechanic and maybe even someday get an automobile dealership. Your dad would have been the perfect mechanic for us."

Ronnie sees Forgione coming down the aisle toward their seats. He turns and walks in that direction, and Boyd follows him, carrying the final hot dog.

"Where can I sit?" Forgione asks Ronnie after Boyd has introduced himself.

Ronnie sits down and pats Boyd's seat, indicating that Forgione should sit there. Both fighters for the main bout are in the ring, prancing and doing warm-up exercises in their robes. Most of the people in the crowd have returned to their seats.

"There's an empty seat over there," Boyd tells them, pointing down the row. "It's been empty all night."

"Would you sit there so I can talk to Forgione for a while?" Ronnie asks him.

"Don't you want this hot dog?" Boyd asks him.

"No, I'm full. You can have it."

"I don't want it," Boyd says.

"Do you want it, Forge?" Ronnie asks. Forgione shakes his head no. There is still sweat on his narrow brow and his hair is wet from his shower. He has remained standing and is watching Boyd. He is holding a brown suède windbreaker in his hand.

"Throw it away then," Ronnie says and turns his attention to Forgione. Boyd walks down the row to the empty seat still carrying the hot dog.

The fighters in the main bout are poorly matched. They are light heavyweights: a lean-muscled Negro from the Roxbury section of Boston and a curly-haired Irish pug from Providence. As the second round draws to a close, the Negro is battering his opponent senseless, while the latter clings to the ropes and refuses to fall. When the bell rings, the Irishman wavers back to his corner, bleeding profusely from his nose and from a cut above his eye. The skin of his stomach is an inflamed pink. The ring doctor and the referee go to his corner, and before the bell can ring for the third round, the fight is stopped.

Ronnie starts immediately down the aisle but Forgione grabs his arm and says:

"Hey, what about your friend?" With his head he indicates Boyd who is working his way down the row.

Ronnie stops and waits for Boyd and the three of them walk slowly with the crowd to the front of the auditorium. In the outer lobby, Ronnie tells them he must make a telephone call and works his way diagonally across the crowd to the phone booths. Boyd follows. Smiling, he says:

"What's her name, Ron?"

"Get my check for me," Ronnie says over his shoulder to Forgione, ignoring Boyd.

Boyd stands alone near the phone booths, and Ronnie watches him while the hospital phone rings. When the switchboard operator answers, he asks her about Jacobs' condition, but she says she must connect him with admissions. Boyd is watching the crowd. Forgione emerges from the box office with one envelope in his hand. He is followed by a woman who holds another envelope in her hand. Forgione points to the phone booth, and when the woman sees Ronnie, she holds his pay envelope in the air. Ronnie slides the door partially open and shouts: "It's O.K., Mrs. Miller. Give it to him." The woman nods and gives the envelope to Forgione, who does a sweeping bow in front of her.

Admissions tells Ronnie they have admitted no one from the fights yet this evening. They give Ronnie the telephone number of a Catholic hospital and tell him to try there. But Jacobs has not been received there yet either. When Ronnie rejoins Forgione and Boyd in the lobby, most of the crowd is gone and a janitor is beginning to sweep away the popcorn boxes, paper cups, cigarette butts and mustard-stained napkins. From the auditorium behind them comes the hollow sound of push-brooms knocking against the tiers of wooden general admission seats.

Outside, a raw, chilling fog has settled over the deep snow piled in yards and along the sides of the streets. The fog dims and diffuses the light from the streetlamps and the marquee of the auditorium.

The three men pause together awkwardly for a moment, and then Boyd says:

"C'mon, Ron. I'll buy you a steak. Or two, if you want them."

"No, thanks," Ronnie says. "I'll eat later. I just had three hot dogs."

"How about you, Jack?" Boyd asks, addressing Forgione. "I'll buy you a steak too. You must be hungry."

"I am," Forgione says.

"Never mind," Ronnie says. "We have to get going."

"How about coming out to the farm," Boyd offers. "Your mother could cook you guys up some big steaks and make a tossed salad. She'd love it."

Ronnie turns away from him. "We'll see you around, Boyd," he says. Forgione starts hesitantly after him.

Boyd takes two strides and grabs Ronnie's elbow. "Please, Ron," he says. "It's like a test. She wants me to bring you back."

Ronnie jerks his elbow away violently. He does not turn to face Boyd but looks down the street and says: "Get lost, Boyd. You're a fucking pest."

Boyd takes the elbow again. "Just one more meal, boy. That's all I'm asking. Jack could stay overnight, and in the morning we could talk about you leaving."

Ronnie jerks the elbow away again, but this time he turns to face Boyd.

"Will you be staying overnight too, Boyd?" he asks.

"Of course not," Boyd tells him.

"You can be honest with me, Boyd. I know you're getting in her pants. I just don't want . . ."

Ronnie is suddenly skidding down the icy sidewalk on his back. The fist that Boyd hit him with is clenched at the big man's side, and Forgione has his chunky arms wrapped tightly around Boyd. Boyd makes no effort to break loose.

Ronnie sits up and feels his jaw. He wipes the back of his hand across his mouth and this time it is bleeding.

"C'mon, Ron," Forgione shouts. "Hit him. I got him."

Ronnie continues to sit on the sidewalk, eyeing Boyd.

"Go ahead, son," Boyd says. "Hit me. I deserve it. I'm sorry."

Ronnie gets slowly to his feet. "Let him go," he tells Forgione.

Forgione releases his grip and backs away. Boyd does not raise his hands as Ronnie approaches him.

Ronnie jabs and hooks with his left hand and Boyd's head snaps to the side. He drives his right fist into the big man's stomach, but Boyd is able to dodge the next right that is aimed at his jaw. Ronnie is enraged and slips to his knee when the wild right misses. Boyd does not attempt to return the fight, but instead backs up slowly with his hands at his sides. Ronnie jabs twice more and Boyd's nose begins to bleed. When Boyd feels the blood trickle down his upper lip, he wipes the back of his hand over it. Ronnie connects with a wild right that drives Boyd back several steps. Ronnie rushes after him, but Boyd blocks another right and knocks Ronnie to the sidewalk again. "That's enough now, boy," Boyd shouts at him. Ronnie's own nose is bleeding now. Again he must tell Forgione not to restrain Boyd. He gets up slowly and then charges at the big man, and again Boyd sends him sprawling with one overpowering swing of his arm. "That's enough," Boyd shouts again. Again Ronnie charges, and again he comes sprawling back into the arms of the crowd gathered around the inside edge of the hot smoky tent. He smells beer on the breath of the man who holds him up. Several other young men beside him with sleeves cut out of their shirts and with tattooes on their sweat-glistening arms throw him back into the makeshift dirt ring. The menacing Negro fighter wearing white silk trunks dances toward him. "Get out there and fight," Hank yells from the crowd. "I got five bucks on you." His shouts sound hollow in the circus tent. Ronnie manages to fall away from a roundhouse punch thrown by the Negro. He is stumbling and it is an immense effort for him to lift his arms. His bare feet are brown from the dusty dirt floor, and the dust clings to his sweaty bare back and to his Levis. The gloves that are tied to his hands are too large and soft to do any damage to the Negro. The pitchman for this tent boxing show ("Stay five minutes, win ten dollars.") is also the referee, and as Ronnie tries to dodge the Negro's blows, the man bumps him constantly. Circling, Ronnie runs into one of the tent posts and as he moves away from it, the Negro hits him in the face with a sledgehammer blow. Ronnie reaches backward and grabs at the crowd for support. He is sure there is some heavy object in his opponent's gloves. Two surly young men push him back into the center of the dirt floor again, sloshing beer on him. The Negro hits him four or five blows in the stomach and then throws a circular uppercut that crushes violently into Ronnie's groin. The men around the edge of the tent give off a collective "ahh!" They begin to hoot and jeer, both at Ronnie who lies writhing in the dust of the tent floor and at the Negro who ducks quickly out the back entrance of the tent. "Who's next?" shouts the pitchman-referee. Hank is the first to reach Ronnie's side and extricate him from the tangled strap that imprisons him in the overturned car. They are in a cornfield and the scene is peaceful and isolated. The corn is high and tassled and the ears on each stalk are almost completely formed. The tumbling car has crushed ten rows of corn in a path that leads back up the steep embankment to the retaining wall on the fourth turn of the Livermore Fairgrounds stock car track. Two men suddenly appear in the gaping hole torn through the wall, and one of them slides down to the wreck. Hank is helping Ronnie inch his way through the window of the crushed car.

"Is he O.K., Hank?" the man shouts, trotting across the flattened cornstalks.

"Just a slight case of rubbery knees," Hank replies as he helps Ronnie to his feet.

"Ah, fuck you," Ronnie says, brushing off his Levis. He smiles but his voice is trembling. Ronnie tries to walk but he stumbles and Hank tightens his grip on the boy's arm. More men appear in the hole above them. One of them shouts:

"How is he?"

"He's all right," Hank tells them. "We're going to sit down for a minute." Ronnie tries to pull away from him, but Hank pushes him down and squats beside him. He lights a cigarette and gives it to Ronnie, who suddenly knows that Hank is proud of what he, Ronnie, has just done: barrel-assed his car to the front of the pack straining for the lead, even though he got flipped for it. They can hear the steady rumble of the stock cars cruising slowly around the track above them.

"I'm sorry about the car," Ronnie says.

Hank begins to grin.

"I am. I'm really sorry," Ronnie insists.

Hank's grin widens until it is a laugh.

"What the hell's so funny. I said I was sorry." Ronnie tries to stand up again, but Hank pulls him down.

"If you could have seen your face," Hank wheezes, almost doubled over with his laughing.

"When?" Ronnie asks seriously.

"When you were upside down."

"You mean just now. In the car."

"Yes," Hank says. "All strapped in and hanging onto the steering wheel so tight I thought your knuckles would break. Like you were on a Sunday drive, cruising along through the field on your roof. I should've left you like that. You looked so content."

Ronnie tries to resist Hank's mirth, but it overwhelms him too until they are both sitting in the cornfield laughing at each other.

When he can speak, Ronnie says: "Again, I'm sorry about the car."

"A car's a car," Hank replies. "It's you I care about. Cars I can fix."

Ronnie stands up and begins to brush dirt from the seat of his pants. "Did you ever flip one like that?" he asks.

"Plenty of times," Hank says.

"In a novice race?" Ronnie asks, taking a last puff on his cigarette and crushing it out with his shoe.

"Sure," Hank replies. "You got to start somewhere."

They scramble up the embankment together, Hank on strong agile legs not yet mangled by the motorcycle accident. When Ronnie emerges onto the track through the hole in the retaining wall, the public address system announces:

"There he is, folks. Looks like he's O.K. Let's give him

a big hand." The crowd applauds and Ronnie's face goes beet-red as they walk across the track.

In the infield after the race has started up again Ronnie hears another driver ask Hank:

"Was that the car you were planning to use in the feature tomorrow?"

"Naw. I got plenty of cars," Hank answers.

Hank and Ronnie work through the afternoon and into the night putting Hank's second car into shape for the feature race the next day. The fair goes on around them, and Ronnie, who has just returned from a graduation trip to Florida, cancels a date so he can help his father with the car. While they work they drink beer and eat hot dogs, fried chicken and corn on the cob. It is ten-thirty when Hank declares the car ready to roll. With the help of some others who are working on cars in the infield, they push-start it and Hank takes it for a few trial laps around the dimly lit track. By the time he returns to the infield, Ronnie has started his motorcycle. Hank drives up beside him, the muffler-less car cracking and growling.

"Where you going?" Hank shouts over the noise. Ronnie revs the motorcycle as he sits astride it.

"Home," he shouts.

Hank cuts the car engine and says: "Hang it up. We'll drink some beer and go see the hootchy-cootch show. They got some real snatch-wavers this year."

Ronnie kills the motorcycle engine.

They walk down a corridor of yellow light coming from the string of bulbs above the tents. The fair is in the middle of a field and the grass under their booted feet is trampled and dusty. They have washed hastily, and their arms and hands are smudged with traces of grease. Grease is clogged under their fingernails. Hank's shirt is unbuttoned and he carries a can of beer from which Ronnie occasionally sips. They have not reached the strip show when a harsh roar from the boxing tent stops them. On the outside is a sign with a crude picture of two boxers, one knocking the other off his feet, with the legend:

O'REILLY'S WORLD CHAMPION BOXERS

A word balloon coming from the champ's mouth, as he knocks his opponent senseless, challenges: "How long can you last?" Admission to the tent is twenty-five cents. Inside, it is hot and dusty, and the prevailing odor is sweat. Over the heads of the shouting men that line the edge of the tent, Ronnie and Hank can see a Negro with long slick hair and green trunks pounding at will on the head of a tough-looking man with a crewcut and tattooes. The man is bare-footed and wears no shirt, and he covers his head with his gloves, now and then coming out of his crouch to try a swing at the Negro. Each time he attempts this, the Negro hits him in the face, until finally he drives him back against the circle of men. When the men try to push him back into the center of the circle, he drops to his knees and wheezes: "Enough."

The referee-pitchman holds the Negro's gloved hand aloft and then quickly dismisses him.

"Who's next?" he shouts. "Ten dollars for five minutes. Can you last?"

"I want to try that," Ronnie says.

"Go ahead," Hank tells him. He flashes a wry grin at Ronnie and takes the beer can from him. "I'd like to see you get your ass kicked."

Ronnie running.

Hup.

Hup.

Hup.

Hup.

Three miles in a dark leaf-strewn park. October sky clear with stars. No moon yet. Ronnie, in gray gym suit and black knit cap. Running. Running enlarges chest muscles. Hearts learns to pump more blood with single stroke—*baloosh.* Slows pulse. Oak leaves wet and frozen white. Frozen grass crust crumbles under foot. Icy puddles. Walk. Drag air. Twenty-three minutes: forty-two seconds. We've broken the eight-minute mile here. Sweat steaming in the frozen night. Jog up the gym steps.

Ronnie on the light bag. Opponent's head.

Bup-a-dit.

Bup-a-dit, bup-a-dit.

Bup-a-d'bup-a-d'bup-a-d'buppadbuppadbuppadbuppadbuppadbuppa. Arms aching. Shake them down. Buppabuppabuppabuppabuppa.

Ronnie on the heavy bag. Opponent's body.

Whump. Dance. Whumpwhump. Whumpwhump. Whumpwhumpwhump.

"Cover, Ronnie."

"What for? It don't hit back." Whumpwhump. Whumpwhumpwhump. Bags swings out. Ronnie moves after it. Whump. Dances back. Bag swinging back. Whump stops it; shudders up his arm.

"You wanna spar, Ronnie?"

"I wanna sit down. Who with?"

"Forgione."

"Yeh, in a minute. Tell the big ape not to kill me."

"O.K."

"Get me a headguard too."

"What size?"

"I don't know. Get Lockhart's. It fits me."

Ape prancing in ring. Rocking the ropes.

"Hi, Ron."

"Hello, Ape. You a middleweight now?"

"No. I got a short opponent. Want to see if I can hit him in the belly."

"You outreach me enough to hit me in the knees. Be careful."

"Three two's, Ron?"

"O.K. with me."

"Arty. Give us a bell. Three two-minute rounds."

"Ronnie, you still got my stopwatch."

"I gave it to Smitty. Use your wrist watch."

"Time."

Heavyweight Forgione more cautious than necessary with 155-pound Ronnie. They circle. Ronnie stretches a left hand that doesn't reach, and Forgione hooks his own left on Ronnie's headguard. Back off. Ape following. Two lefts in Ronnie's face. Ronnie blocks stomach-right with elbow, pushes his own right in Ape's face, slides out of corner. Easy round. Feel and circle. Circle and feel.

"Time."

Ronnie stands in corner holding mouthpiece. Refuses water.

"Time."

Forgione tattooing Ronnie's head. Ronnie moves inside wide hook, clinches.

"Hey, Ape. Easy. I got a date and I want to be able to kiss her good night."

They push off. Ronnie swings wild right. Misses. Slips. Forgione offers hand to get up. Ronnie takes. Slaps Ape's head. Dances back. Laughing. Ape not laughing. Moving in. Ronnie sticks two straight lefts on his nose. Stops Ape. Ronnie out. In again. Feints left. Belts right.

"Time."

Ronnie takes water now. People moving over to watch.

"Time."

Ronnie annoying Ape. Sticking lefts. In and out. Covering head. Taking it in gut. Good for stomach. Like medicine ball. Big Ape target. Ronnie moves in. Infight mix-up. Ape getting best of it. Head head. Stomach stomach. Ronnie jabs left. Starts to throw right. And is sitting on his ass.

"Time."

Ape laughing. Is nose bleeding? Arm wipe check reveals no. Ape helping him up again. Ronnie grins.

Ronnie on weights. Tired now. Neck work. Bench presses. That's enough for now. Nose sore. Legs tired. Arms all gone. Sit-ups. Ninety-eight. Ninety-agh-nine. Hundred-ahh.

Ronnie in shower. Eyes shut. Head bent. Boiling nape and shoulders. Hip wound aching. Thighs begging him to sit down. Running soapy hands over steel stomach. Hard biceps, thighs, calves.

Cold outside. Hair wet. Stars replaced by light snow falling on the leaves. Rush of warm air from the taproom. Smell of steam heat, metal. Malt. Muscles tingle. Slouch in padded booth. Perfume in her hair. Touch thighs lightly.

Boyd's punch drives a nail from Ronnie's jaw into the back of his head. A shower of sparks explodes behind his eyelids. His head cracks the ice on the sidewalk, driving the nail back across the top of his skull to his forehead.

Ronnie rolls over on his stomach and draws his knees under himself. He kneels erect, wavers, and braces his fists against the ice. He looks for Boyd in the spinning fog crystal night but sees only the crowd around him. There are spots of blood on the sidewalk beneath him. He stumbles to his feet and before he can fall he is in the firm restraining grip of Forgione. He struggles faintly but Forgione tells him he has had enough. The fight is over. He locates Boyd who is standing with his back to a group of onlookers. Boyd is breathing hard, almost sobbing, with his head bent down and his fists clenched at his sides. When Ronnie sees Boyd he struggles again but Forgione squeezes him tightly and says again that the fight is over. Ronnie calms down. He turns his head over his shoulder and says:

"Let's get out of here, Forge."

"Where's your car?" Forgione asks. He does not release his grip.

"Down the street." Ronnie nods to the area behind Forgione.

"I'm sorry, Ron," Boyd says. His head is still bent and his cowboy hat covers his eyes. "You made me do it."

Forgione tightens his grip, but Ronnie does not resist him.

"You cowboy clown," Ronnie says slowly, contemptuously. "My old man would have killed you."

"I'm sorry," Boyd mumbles. He still has not looked up.

"You fucking cowboy." Ronnie's voice raises to a shout. "You *mother*fucking cowboy. You *mother*fucker. Mother*fuckerrrrrrrr.*"

Forgione turns him quickly and marches him down the street.

# V

Look at Ronnie Mandeville. He is seated in his dark blue 1949 Ford examining his battered face in the rear-view mirror. The car is cold, but the motor is running. Ronnie pumps the gas pedal unconsciously while he looks at the face, and the car crackles and snarls in its parking place on the snow-filled street. Beside Ronnie sits his friend, Jack Forgione, who watches him silently. The night is foggy and damp, and the chill from the cold mist penetrates to the bone. Both fighters are overheated, and the windows of the car began to fog over almost as soon as they entered the car. The light from the streetlamp that illuminates Ronnie's face is softened by the heavy fog.

Blood and mucus stream from Ronnie's nose, and as he watches the mirror's image, he cleans the nose with a handkerchief. He thinks the nose may be broken, and he squeezes the bridge gingerly with his index finger and his thumb. It is swelling slightly, but not nearly as much as the lump over his left eye. This swelling expands the old scar that splits his eyebrow. It also pushes flesh down over the corner of his eye, partially obscuring his vision. His mouth, from which a tooth has been missing for six years, is also bleeding. There is a thin slit just below the line of the lower lip both inside and outside the mouth where one of his bottom teeth punctured the flesh that was driven over it by Boyd's first punch. The blood coming from this wound is negligible and can be blotted both inside and out with the handkerchief. Forgione's handkerchief is wrapped around a melting snowball that Ronnie holds against the base of his skull to help stop the flow of blood from his nose. There is a rapidly swelling lump where the back of Ronnie's head hit the icy sidewalk. Next to this lump, but covered by Ronnie's long brown hair, is a small white scar where Ronnie's head was cut open by a fall against the edge of a car door during a fight with his father. Other disfigurations on his body include three red swollen knuckles on his left hand, an appendectomy scar, a red "RON" on a blue banner tattooed on his left shoulder, and a jagged blue scar on his right hip, fatter on one end than the other.

After Ronnie has stared at himself for some time, moving his head left and right and up and down to view different sections of his face in the tiny mirror, Forgione reaches across and takes the soggy ice pack from him and continues to hold it gently against Ronnie's neck. With his other hand, Forgione presses Ronnie's forehead away from the mirror so that his head reclines against the seat.

Ronnie is still breathing hard. The pain makes his eyes water, and as Forgione withdraws his hands and leaves him resting against the seat, the water in his eyes overflows and a drop runs down each side of his cheek. Ronnie dabs quickly at these drops with the bloody handkerchief. The blood that has fallen on his green sweater is a dull black under the soft light of the streetlamp.

When the blood in his nose has clotted, Ronnie cleans his face as best as he can with the wet, snow-filled handkerchief. Forgione asks him if he wants to go to the hospital to get the puncture in his lower lip stitched or to have the nose X-rayed. Ronnie says no, and holding the wet ice pack against the puncture, puts the car in gear with his free hand and guns it out of the snow-rutted parking space into the slick street. He travels only two blocks and then guides the car into a gas station lot, parking at the dark side near the rest rooms. A huge pile of snow has been plowed into a hill that stretches along the back edge of the lot all the way to the street. Children have used this man-made hill for sliding, and several makeshift sleds of squashed boxes or single sheets of cardboard are scattered around. Ronnie pulls on the emergency brake but leaves the motor running. Clutching both his handkerchief and Forgione's he goes to the men's room door. Forgione stays in the car. Ronnie rattles the door, but it is locked, and he returns and asks Forgione if he will get the key from the station attendant. While he is waiting, Ronnie shuts off the car's engine and takes his keys from the ignition switch. He opens the trunk of the Ford and removes his suitcase, which he takes into the men's room with him when Forgione returns with the key. When Ronnie comes back, his swollen face is scrubbed clean and his hair is once more slicked down with water. He has changed into a navy-blue V-neck sweater. He carries the suitcase, into which he has thrown the bloody sweater, in his right hand and the two freshly washed handkerchiefs balled up in his left hand. The men's room key is his back pocket, and when he gives it to Forgione to return, he asks the husky fighter to see if he can buy a small tin of aspirin tablets in the gas station. Ronnie tosses the suitcase on the back seat. Forgione returns with aspirin and Ronnie takes three and swallows them dry. He starts the car engine.

"Where do you want me to take you?" he asks Forgione.

"I thought we were going to get something to eat," Forgione says, turning to face him.

"I'm not hungry," Ronnie says. "I want to get going." He pumps the gas pedal nervously.

"Where are you going? Home?"

"No. Away."

"Out of state?"

"Yeh."

"Tonight?"

"As soon as I take you where you want to go."

"Where are you going?" Forgione repeats.

Ronnie points to the Route One sign on the other side of the gas station lot and says:

"I'm going to get on that big old conveyor belt, and I'm not going to get off until it dumps me on the beach at Key West." When he turns to look at Forgione, he must tilt his head slightly to see him through his swollen eye.

"You ought to get a night's sleep if you're going to do all that driving."

"Why don't you go along? We'll take turns driving and sleeping. We can do it in a day and a half. I did it after I graduated high school."

"I got to go to work tomorrow."

"No you don't. You said your uncle always gives you the day off after a fight."

"Well, I got to go the next day anyway."

"Quit. You can get a job in Florida. There's a lot more construction work down there than there is here."

"I can't quit. My mother would kill me."

"Well, I'm going. Where do you want me to drop you off?"

"If I don't get something to eat, I'm going to turn inside out. Have a steak with me and then take off. You'll feel better."

"I want to go now. I'm not hungry."

"You should eat something. You'll be eating cheese crackers and candy and all kinds of junk on the road, and that's not good for your stomach. Just have a hamburger and a beer. You have to eat."

"All right," Ronnie says. He puts the car in gear and pulls out of the gas station lot. "I guess I am hungry."

"Maybe you'll change your mind about getting some sleep first too," Forgione tells him. "My mother could fix you a nice big breakfast, and you could get a fresh start in the morning."

The beer is soothing as it flows over Ronnie's punctured lip. Draft beer that stays cold all the way into his stomach. From the first sip, he relaxes. The back room of the restaurant-bar is less than half-filled with diners. From the booth in which they sit facing each other they can see most of the tables and watch the waitresses, who wear pink uniforms and black aprons. The padded booth is soft and Ronnie is sore but comfortable. On the table between the two fighters is a pitcher of beer, and Ronnie pours his second glass from it. It comes over him that he has made a total break from his home and that he is free. Freer than he has ever been. And the first sign of his freedom was winning an important fight. He takes the hundred-dollar check from his shirt pocket and looks at it. In two days he will be in Florida, away from the ice and snow. He plans to loll around on the beaches for a week or two, as long as the money holds out, before he gets a job. Across the dining room is an open doorway leading to the bar. It is a brightly lighted room, and Ronnie can see the drinkers seated on bar stools. Through the doorway comes their waitress, carrying Forgione's steak and Ronnie's hamburger. She places the dishes on the table and gets a bottle of ketchup from the table behind her and places it near Ronnie. As she is picking up Forgione's empty salad plate, Ronnie says:

"Can I have a steak, please? Sirloin, the same as that." He nods at Forgione's plate.

"Certainly, sir," the waitress says. She puts the plate down and draws her order book and pencil from her apron pocket. "Medium rare also?" she asks, already writing it down.

"But Roquefort on the salad," Ronnie says.

"Yes, sir." She stares at Ronnie's battered face longer than she should, and Ronnie drops his eyes. She picks up the salad plate again and turns to leave. Forgione stops her, struggling the words through a mouthful of steak:

"I want another steak too. Same thing. Skip the salad."

She replaces the plate, withdraws the book and pencil again and adds the order. Ronnie laughs at her coldness and at Forgione for ordering another steak, but she doesn't react. She replaces the book and pencil, picks up the plate for the third time, pivots quickly toward the bar and leaves. Ronnie turns his full attention to his hamburger which he finishes by the time she returns with his salad. Forgione pours the last beer from the pitcher and orders more. By the time she brings their steaks they have drained half of their second pitcher. They finish their steaks quickly. With his stomach full and the beer working on him, Ronnie becomes drowsy. The waitress brings coffee, but Forgione does not want his, so Ronnie drinks both cups, as well as another glass of beer.

"I've really got to go," he says, draining his glass.

"Go where?" Forgione asks, pouring off the remaining beer in the pitcher. "You'll be asleep before you hit Boston." Forgione gulps down the beer and stands up. "C'mon," he says, "Let's go to Sportsman's and have the fight fans buy us some drinks."

"Naw, I really want to leave," Ronnie says.

Shouts and smoke-filled air greet them inside Sportsman's. Ronnie switches to Scotch and has three doubles on the rocks without touching his wallet. Several times he must demonstrate the combination of punches that knocked Jacobs unconscious, each time on a willing partner who feigns the stiff, damaged posture Jacobs assumed after the punches fell. Almost everyone who talks to Ronnie questions him about his battered face, saying they did not realize he had taken so much punishment. Ronnie is anxious to preserve the idea that he had an easy time with his opponent, so he tells them hurriedly about the fight on the street, emphasizing the fact that he was outweighed by at least eighty pounds. "If you think I look bad," he tells them, "you should see the other guy." Forgione backs him up on this, and they laugh, but in truth Ronnie knows that Boyd's features have not been altered at all by his fists. The big man's nose had already stopped bleeding when Ronnie was still picking himself up from the icy street. Boyd will look no different when he returns to Virginia Jane, and consequently, he will not have to explain anything to her. But Ronnie knows he will, good Christian soul that he is; that he will describe his fight with his mistress' only son; and that he will be forgiven by Virginia Jane since Virginia Jane has no other choice now.

Ronnie is offered a cigarette and he takes it, holding it

in his mouth until a light is offered. In response to a question, Ronnie tells the group that the fight on the street was over a personal matter.

"Oh yeah," says a crewcut, beer-bellied veteran of the Second World War. "What's her name?"

"This cigarette tastes terrible," Ronnie says. He drops it to the floor, steps on it and crushes back his long brown hair with his hand. He takes a large gulp of whiskey from the short glass on the bar in front of him. "I've got to go pretty soon," he says.

Ronnie takes a large gulp from the short glass of whiskey in front of him on the table. They are in a hotel lounge seated at a table at the edge of a low stage. A comedian is finishing his act. The audience applauds lightly. The master of ceremonies comes out and introduces "two well-known pugilists in the audience tonight, both local boys, Jack Forgione, the heavyweight, and Donnie Mandeville, the middleweight. Stand up, boys."

"Ronnie," Ronnie shouts, standing up to the applause.

"Ronnie," the man on stage repeats. "I'm sorry. Both these boys, I understand, knocked their opponents senseless tonight and are here for a little celebration. Right, boys?"

Ronnie and Forgione sit down and hold their drinks aloft to more applause. Ronnie sees the curtains part slightly at the rear of the stage. The eye that looks through the slit is feminine and heavily made-up. Ronnie feels it is looking directly at him.

"Where does this guy get his information?" Ronnie asks, leaning across the table to Forgione.

"I told him when we came in," Forgione says. "My uncle owns part of this place."

Ronnie turns back to the slit in the curtains through

which a very pale leg has appeared, exposed to the top of the thigh and wearing a shiny red spike-heeled shoe. A spotlight suddenly falls on the leg, catching also a piece of the master of ceremonies who is now dashing off stage. The drummer in the three-piece combo to the right of the stage begins to stomp on his bass drum, and the trombonist slides his instrument back and forth with exaggerated insinuation. The leg is followed by the rest of the stripper, tightly wrapped in a long silk sheath of red, slit on the side to expose the teasing leg. The face under a short boyish helmet of blond hair looks directly at Ronnie. Ronnie grins and then quickly rubs the back of his hand over his mouth. The bass drum and the trombone continue their introduction while the stripper struts with professional grace around the edge of the stage. When she reaches Ronnie's table, she stops, and bending down, takes Ronnie's swollen face in her hands. He flinches slightly because her thumb touches the bridge of his nose, and then she kisses him wetly on the lips, releasing him perfunctorily and spinning away to the back of the stage where she begins to caress her thighs and the mound in the middle of the sheath. The bare leg flashes through the slit several times and she also caresses this with her hands and arms that are clothed in long red velvet gloves. Each time the hand reaches the top of the pale smooth thigh it is magnetically drawn—against even her wishes, so it would seem—to the mound underneath the dress. This autoerotic suggestion creates an irresistible urge in Ronnie to touch his private parts. Just a scratch or a friendly rub to let them know they have not been forgotten. But he does not move a muscle, except to gulp occasionally at his drink. Not even when the stripper is naked—shaved and naked but for three negligible smidgens of cloth, and Ronnie can smell the soft perfume she uses on her body and see the glistening sweat in her hairless armpits and feel the smooth pale comfortable care she takes of her flesh—does he move. Not a muscle. Not a muscle moves even when the entire sweet nakedness is at the exact edge of the stage, bent and hovering over his table, vibrating its creamy pale shoulders and arms so that its dangling taut breasts rumble and flap less than six inches from Ronnie's punctured lip. The baby draws the nipple greedily into its mouth, its nose pressed tightly into the bulging soft flesh of Virginia Jane's breast. Ronnie draws Bunnie's nipple greedily into his mouth draws the stripper's perfumed breast greedily into his mouth draws Bunnie's entire adolescent breast into his mouth. But Ronnie still does not move a muscle. Even though his penis fills rapidly with blood and presses painfully against his fly. Now the stripper is gone back through the curtain and Ronnie moves a muscle that lifts his arm to reach for his drink that lifts the drink to his punctured lip and pours what remains in the glass into his mouth. Greedily.

In the next place, there are five musicians on a platform: three standing electric guitarists, plus a seated drummer and a stand up/sit down electric organist. Each has a microphone angled in at his face so he can sing or shout while torturing his instrument, and each has shoulder-length hair that bounces and snaps from side to side as they rock to the beat they have created. Ronnie and Forgione stand at the back of the hall drawing in greedily the sight of young girls flailing and jumping with their partners on the large central dance floor. Lights swirl and flash on the couples from the stage and from the corners of the hall. The sound out of the huge speakers is deafening, but Ronnie is trying to finish a conversation he started in the car on the way from the hotel lounge.

"Cus D'Amato is looking for a middleweight to manage," he screams, leaning close to Forgione's ear.

"What?" Forgione turns to look at Ronnie.

Ronnie repeats his statement. Forgione points to Ronnie and asks: "You?"

"Why not?" Ronnie shouts.

"Who told you?"

"Smitty," Ronnie answers, referring to the club manager.

The music stops abruptly, as Forgione yells into the silence: "How does he know?"

"That's what he said," Ronnie answers softly.

"What does a big name like that want with a middleweight?"

"He wants to groom him for the championship."

"Are you going to do it?" Forgione has an astonished look on his face, as if he is already imagining Ronnie, who is less than mediocre, as middleweight champion of the world.

"He doesn't want me, you big clod." Ronnie laughs. "He's shopping around, and I made a good show tonight. But he wasn't even there."

"He'll hear about it."

"I'll be in Florida if he wants me," Ronnie says.

The music starts again, sending out sound waves which they can actually feel vibrating against their faces. Neither fighter makes a move to find a table, and both lean against the wall near the door, watching the dancing which has started again under the flashing lights in the center of the room. After a few minutes Ronnie shouts:

"Let's sit down. I want a beer." Only beer—plus soft drinks for teen-agers—is served in this hall, and a state law forbids any alcoholic beverages to be consumed standing up.

Forgione is no stranger here, and he greets people in the young crowd as the two fighters work their way to a vacant table near the dance floor. They sit down, facing the dancers, and while waiting to be served, they avoid touching the sticky glasses, the spilled beer and ashes on their table.

"Who was the one you said hello to?" Ronnie shouts to Forgione.

"She goes with my cousin," Forgione replies.

"Is your cousin here?"

"No."

"Invite her over."

"My cousin wouldn't like it."

The music stops again, and Ronnie stands up. "Order a beer for me," he tells Forgione. "I'm going to make a phone call."

"Don't call any girls," Forgione says. "There's plenty here."

"I'm going to call the hospital."

Forgione frowns but nods his approval, and Ronnie leaves the table and works his way back through the crowd to a telephone booth. The door of the booth does not shut out the noise from the band, and when Ronnie gets through to the hospital he cannot hear what the nurse on the other end of the line tells him. He hangs up and goes outside to look for a phone booth on the street. The fog has condensed into a freezing rain, and a sheet of ice coats the parked cars, parking meters and the sidewalk. He doesn't see a telephone so he ducks quickly back into the smoky hall and returns to the table.

The table has been cleaned and Forgione sits with a full glass of beer in front of him.

"How is he?" he shouts when Ronnie reaches the table.

"I couldn't hear the nurse for all the fucking noise," Ronnie leans over and screams at him. "Where's my beer?"

For an answer, Forgione nods to the waitress who is standing behind Ronnie's chair.

"May I see your draft card, please?" she asks Ronnie.

She does not raise her voice, but for some reason Ronnie can hear her clearly through the electric sounds. He withdraws his wallet from his rear pocket and takes from it his discharge papers. Ronnie is angry and Forgione, who is watching him with amusement, leans back in his chair and says to the waitress:

"Do you want to dance, honey?"

"I ain't allowed to while I'm working," she tells him and turns to examining Ronnie's papers. She leans over the table, holding her serving tray and rag at her side.

"How about after work?" Forgione continues.

"Maybe," she says. She smiles at him and pushes the certificate back across the table to Ronnie.

"Why do you want to pick up a pig like that?" Ronnie asks after she has gone. They turn to watch her work her way through the crowd taking orders. She is heavy and perhaps in her mid-twenties and wears black stretch ski pants and a black sleeveless turtleneck jersey that molds tightly over her enormous breasts and also over the roll of fat around her middle. Her face is pretty in a sweet way but the heaviness shows there too, and her smooth fair complexion and large eyes seem stark in contrast to her dyed black hair.

"That's the reserve fund," Forgione tells him. "If we can't do any better, we've always got that to keep us warm. I bet she has lots of friends too."

"Every one of them built like her," Ronnie says.

The girl brings Ronnie's glass of beer, for which Forgione has already paid. "Don't forget us now," Forgione says.

"I won't," she says and hurries away.

"We also get better service," Forgione says to Ronnie who is taking a large swallow of his beer. "It never hurts anyone to smile at an ugly girl."

But Ronnie is not listening to him. He is slowly lowering his glass to the table and staring at the dance floor. Forgione tries to follow his stare, but he cannot tell what has drawn Ronnie's attention.

"See the blonde?" Ronnie asks. He does not take his eyes from the dance floor.

"Wow, yeah," Forgione explains. "What a piece of ass. Wouldn't you like to screw that with no questions asked?"

"That's my sister," Ronnie says without looking at Forgione.

"Oh," the big fighter says, sitting forward. After a pause, he adds: "She's a fantastic dancer, Ron."

And Bunnie *is* a fantastic dancer. She is still wearing her tiny suède skirt but now she has on tights the color of dark flesh, knee-high brown vinyl boots, and a white blouse with an excess of ruffles down the front and at the wrists. She wears huge lollypop sunglasses and her hair streams from side to side in the flashing lights as she flails her arms and bobs her head and body to the rhythms of the music. She is dancing with a man who is more a spectator than a partner since he stands as far from her as the crowded dance area will allow. The man has curly black hair, sideburns and a bushy mustache. Like Bunnie, he is wearing sunglasses, and he alternately claps his hands and snaps his fingers while grinning encouragement to her. As Ronnie watches, the tempo of the music slows and the man moves to Bunnie and wraps his arms around her waist with his hands placed suggestively near the top of the tiny skirt. Bunnie drapes her arms over the man's shoulders and their bodies press together and move to the slowly surging beat of the music. Ronnie stands up quickly and walks between two tables to the dance floor. Forgione leans back in his chair, takes a swallow of beer and keeps his eyes on Ronnie.

When Ronnie reaches them, he taps Bunnie on the

shoulder and asks her if she wants to dance. The man looks up first and says:

"No."

Ignoring Ronnie, he presses his face to Bunnie's long blond hair with his mouth at her ear.

Bunnie draws her head away from this gesture of affection and turns it slowly to face Ronnie. Her eyes are hidden behind the large sunglasses but Ronnie can see her looking absently at him, trying to place his familiar but battered face. Suddenly she squeals his name, pushes the clinging man away and throws her arms around her brother's neck.

"My brother," she explains quickly to the man, who is already moving toward Ronnie. "The one I was telling you about."

"Oh," the man says. He takes the hand that Ronnie has extended around Bunnie.

"Nice to meet you," Ronnie says.

"I'll be at the table," the man tells Bunnie. He turns and picks a path through the couples on the dance floor.

Ronnie draws Bunnie to him, and with their bodies touching lightly, they begin to dance.

"Wow, what are you doing here?" she asks, speaking rapidly, "I was just thinking about you, and then suddenly there you were. I couldn't believe it. It's like I made you up with my mind. Poof, and you tap me on the shoulder."

"Have you been drinking?" Ronnie asks accusingly.

"I'm on my sixth Coke," she says.

"You sure sound like you've been drinking."

"And you sure smell like you have."

"I'm old enough."

"Just barely."

"Who's the creep you were dancing with?"

"A friend. And he's not a creep. He's cool."

"Is he the one you came to meet?"

"Yes."

"How old is he?"

"Twenty-nine."

"What?" Ronnie asks in amazement. "I thought you said he was nineteen."

"I was afraid you'd tell mother."

"What makes you think I won't tell her now?"

"You're not going back, are you?"

Ronnie does not answer her. Instead he draws her thin body tightly against himself so that he can feel the distinct outline of her thighs as they press against his own.

"Hey, what are you doing?" Bunnie laughs nervously and pushes him with her left hand which she has been resting on his shoulder. Ronnie releases her and she backs away to a more comfortable position as they continue to dance. The conversation does not begin again. Ronnie stares into Bunnie's face through his headache and his reddened eyes, through the whiskey and beer he has been drinking for the last couple of hours.

"I heard about your fight," she says. "I think it's fabulous that you got a knockout."

Ronnie does not answer her.

"It's too bad about your face," she continues. "I've never seen you so beat up. It must have been a good fight."

Ronnie releases her hand, which he has been holding in the proper dancing pose, and places both his palms on the tight suède-covered cheeks of her buttocks. Before she can protest, he draws her roughly to him, so that the lower half of their bodies collide violently.

"Ronnie, stop it," she hisses with anger. She reaches behind herself and raises his hands to her waist. Ronnie accepts this but continues to pull on her waist, keeping their bodies locked together.

"Behave yourself," Bunnie tells him. She tugs again at his wrists, but when she cannot move them, she places her hands on his shoulders, accepting the body contact rather than make a disturbance on the dance floor. The music surges on, and as they move together with it, Ronnie says:

"I thought you met that guy at a basketball game."

"I did," Bunnie answers with resentment.

"Isn't he kind of old to be going to a high school game?"

"He likes teen-agers. Most of his friends are my age."

"I'll bet he's married," Ronnie says.

"So what?" Bunnie says contemptuously.

"Is he?"

"Yes. But he's separated," Bunnie tells him, and then adds quickly: "Everybody's entitled to one mistake."

"How many kids does he have?"

"I don't know," Bunnie says. Her eyes drop sheepishly.

"How many?" Ronnie squeezes her waist for emphasis.

"Two."

"That's three mistakes," Ronnie says. He eases his grip on her waist and she backs away slightly.

"So what?" she repeats. Now she looks up at Ronnie defiantly. "He's a cool guy. And he's good to his friends. And to me."

Ronnie suddenly drops his hands to her buttocks again and slams her body to his.

"Will you stop it!" she screams. She pushes at his chest.

Ronnie does not release her or remove his hands from her buttocks. Instead he begins to move his body suggestively against hers.

"Please stop it," she says. Her hands are still pressed against his chest in resistance. As she leans back away from him, the top half of his body leans forward to follow her.

"Just pretend I'm your boy friend," Ronnie tells her, his lips searching for her evasive mouth.

Bunnie reaches up suddenly and slaps him. The music covers the noise of the slap, although some couples on the dance floor see it and turn their heads to watch them. Ronnie drops his grip, and they stand facing each other silently. Bunnie is the first one to move. She places both her hands on Ronnie's cheeks and says:

"I'm sorry. I really am. I didn't mean it."

The slap seems to have calmed Ronnie. "How did you get here?" he says to her.

"Boyd dropped me off on his way to the fight."

"Boyd?" Ronnie asks in astonishment. They face each other for a moment before Ronnie begins to laugh. "Boyd?" he repeats. Bunnie turns to walk away from him and his laugh stops abruptly. He grabs her wrist and spins her around to face him.

"I'm taking you home," he says. "You're as bad as your goddamned mother. You'll be knocked up by nineteen like she was." He begins to drag her off the dance floor. She resists but he is much stronger and she has little choice. More people turn to watch them.

Halfway between the dance floor and the door, Bunnie stops her resistance. She moves up beside her hurrying brother and shouts:

"Man, you are incredible. *You are bringing me down!*"

Ronnie stops abruptly. "I'm doing *what?*" he screams, asking her to repeat what he knows she has said.

"You are bringing me *down!*" Bunnie repeats.

"Down from where?" Ronnie asks, scrutinizing her face.

Bunnie's friend is now beside her. "You know where from, man," he says, pulling Ronnie's hand away from Bunnie's wrist.

"Did she get it from you?" Ronnie asks, turning to him.

"She knows where to get it."

"What is it?"

"It's just a little smoke, man. Don't get excited."

Ronnie's right hand, its palm open flat, lashes out and slaps the side of the man's head, sending his sunglasses in an arc over several tables and then to the floor where one of the lenses shatters. The man is stunned by the surprise blow, but he recovers quickly and tosses a punch at Ronnie's face with his right hand. Ronnie, with his boxer's instinct, draws his head back deftly to avoid the punch. He coils another punch of his own, but before he can throw it, Forgione is between them. The big fighter wraps one of his massive arms around the man's head and with his free hand he grabs a bunch of the material at the front of Ronnie's sweater and begins to push him backwards toward the door.

At the back of the hall, a door opens and a squat neckless man with a scarred crewcut and a scowl on his face rushes toward the disturbance. He wears a white tee shirt and as he trots through the curious crowd, he brandishes a policeman's billy club.

The four figures—Ronnie, back-pedaling, cooperating with Forgione; Forgione himself, leaning forward to drag the man locked under his arm; the man struggling but off balance, his face under Forgione's arm popping red with his struggle, his arms flailing at Forgione's huge back; and Bunnie running alongside, one hand over her mouth in horror—these four are near the door when the chunky man with the club reaches them.

"Angelo," Forgione barks at him, stopping the arm with the billy club that is about to fall upon the group of them. "It's me, Angelo. I can take care of it." Forgione does not stop his struggle toward the door.

"Oh, it's you, Jackie," the man replies, trotting beside

the group. He does not lower the club. "What's the problem?"

"Nothing. I can handle it. Get the door."

Angelo sprints for the front door and throws it open, bowing slightly and pointing to the street with his billy club as the struggling group jams through it and pops out onto the ice-covered sidewalk.

"Another uncle?" Ronnie asks him, still back-pedaling.

"Cousin," Forgione says, and with a grunt releases Ronnie and shoves him back against a parked car.

Bunnie rushes at Ronnie and tries to restrain him. She shouts: "Don't fight. Please, don't fight. Bo can't fight. He's too stoned."

Ronnie pushes her aside when Forgione releases his captive. The man takes a wild swing at Forgione, and then locates Ronnie and charges him. Ronnie ducks and spins away from the first wild punch, and the man skids to the parked car, his arms working desperately to maintain his balance. Ronnie moves to the middle of the sidewalk, dancing lightly on the balls of his feet, and when the man charges him again, he stops him with a left jab that lands squarely on the man's nose. Ronnie slides quickly forward and hooks another left on the side of the man's head, and then shifting all his weight to his left foot and swinging his right leg forward, he crosses the man with a right that lands crisply on his jaw and snaps him backward and down to the sidewalk. It all takes just about a second, and the fight is over. Curious people are still hurrying through the door of the dance hall to gather at the edge of the crowd that forms in a semicircle around the fight. Some of them stretch sweaters or jackets over their heads as makeshift umbrellas against the rain.

The man seems more astonished than hurt. He sits on the sidewalk watching Ronnie in wide-eyed wonder and rubbing his jaw. Bunnie kneels beside him and asks him if he is all right. The man shrugs and then cautiously gets to his feet, brushing at the wet spot on the seat of his pants. Ronnie, his fists clenched, watches him narrowly.

"Let's get out of here," the man tells Bunnie. "Go get my jacket and your coat."

Bunnie glances at Ronnie and then pushes through the crowd. Neither Ronnie nor the man look at each other now. Both concentrate on the ice cover of the sidewalk, and Ronnie chips at the ice with the toe of his shoe. The crowd begins to file back through the doorway of the hall, and soon only the three men remain on the sidewalk, illuminated by the streetlights and by the dim flashing colors coming through the windows of the hall. Forgione stands close to Ronnie. He watches the other man carefully, while Ronnie seems to pay no attention to him, concentrating instead on chipping patterns in the ice at his feet. The man stands perfectly still waiting for Bunnie. His head is bowed and his hands are folded in front of him. The rain ticks against the storefront windows and against the parked cars that are rapidly losing their shapes and colors beneath the growing coat of ice. Columns of ice grow against the bricks of the buildings and hang from the ledges and apartment windows and from the sign that sways in the wind above the dance hall. Bunnie returns and for a moment the four of them stand in embarrassed silence. The man puts on the jacket Bunnie hands him. She is already wearing her short coat and clutching a purse.

"Did you find my sunglasses?" the man asks, drawing the coat over his shoulders.

"They're broken," Bunnie says.

"Oh," he replies.

And that is all. They turn and Bunnie takes the man's

arm as they walk away. Ronnie looks up but continues to toe at the ice. They walk under a streetlight in the glitter of the falling ice and rain, and then they are gone.

"Let's go have another beer," Ronnie says, heading toward the door of the dance hall.

"Why don't we go over to my house and get something to eat?" Forgione suggests.

"Because I want to drink," Ronnie tells him.

Forgione shrugs and they go back to the dance hall, where Angelo is waiting for them. He blocks the doorway and slaps the palm of his hand with the billy club.

"What's the problem?" Forgione asks him.

"He can't come in," Angelo says, pointing to Ronnie and tapping him lightly on the chest with the club.

"He's with me," Forgione says.

"You can come in if you want, but he can't." Angelo folds his arms with the billy club raised to his shoulder.

"Did you go to the fights tonight?" Forgione asks, changing tack.

"You know I was there. You saw me," Angelo answers.

"Well, this is Ronnie Mandeville, who got the knockout in the bout before me."

"Oh yeh." A smile breaks across Angelo's face. "I didn't recognize you." He switches the billy club to his left hand and thrusts a meaty palm at Ronnie. Ronnie takes it and they shake hands. "You sure showed that kid from Jersey a trick or two. I been watching fights for twenty-five years and I don't think I ever saw a guy fall so hard as tonight." He looks carefully at Ronnie, taking note for the first time of his battered face. "Say," he exclaims. "I didn't know you took such a beating."

"He didn't," Forgione says. "He's been fighting people all over Portland tonight, and one of them got the best of him."

"It wasn't this joker out on the street just now," Angelo says. "I seen that one. You had an easy time."

"No, this was another one," Forgione says. "Earlier. Now, are you going to let us in out of the rain, or do we have to fight *you*?" Forgione jabs at Angelo's huge stomach and then cuffs his ear lightly, sliding his arm around the man's thick head and squeezing it playfully.

"O.K., come on in," Angelo says, pretending to clobber Forgione with the billy club. "But no more fights in here. Understand?"

"Sure," Ronnie tells him. "I don't want to fight any-more."

Angelo moves aside and they step into the smoky noise of the bar. The door swings shut on the falling rain.

# VI

Look at Ronnie Mandeville. He is seated in his dark blue 1949 Ford examining his battered face in the rear-view mirror. The car is warm and the motor is running. Ronnie pumps the gas pedal unconsciously while he stares at the face, moving his head left and right and up and down to view different sections of it in the tiny mirror. Beside him on the seat sits a blond girl, the approximate size, shape and coloring of Bunnie, but older and harder. In the dim light coming from the radio her features are softened by the cushion of blond hair that falls over the shoulders of her open blouse to the tips of her small white breasts. She sits with her back to the passenger door, waiting patiently, smoking a freshly lit cigarette, while Ronnie examines his face and wipes the swollen drop of blood away from the puncture below his lower lip with a damp handkerchief. To see the puncture in the mirror, he must raise himself from the seat with one hand and put his lips within inches of the rectangular mirror, so that his lips fill the glass. The bleeding has stopped, and he sits back in his seat, his arms resting on the steering wheel. He knows the girl is watching him, waiting; knows that her left leg is tucked up on the seat, exposing long portions of white thighs and an even whiter glimpse of her underpants. He looks at her, at the unbuttoned blouse, at her bare breasts which are touched lightly by the ends of her long hair, at the flat expanse of her stomach, at her thin neck, and at the smear of blood—his own—below her lower lip.

"There's some on you," he tells her, leaning across the seat to wipe it away.

When he touches her, she pushes his hand away.

"Oo, your handkerchief is wet," she says. "And cold."

"I had some ice in it earlier. It's clean," he lies.

She allows him to wipe the blood away.

The rain, and the ice that falls with the rain, ticks against the car's roof and hood. The doors of the car are shut and locked, and the windows are rolled up, but the icy tick of the rain comes through the muffled metallic whine of the radio inside the car. This whine is punctuated regularly by outbursts from a disc jockey whose words all run together in a jumble, but whose flexed enthusiasms dart and bound through the darkness.

Ronnie, who is still leaning toward the blonde, drops the bloody wet handkerchief to the floor and touches her exposed breast. She flinches involuntarily, and he kisses her lightly on the lips.

"Did the blood stop?" she asks.

"Yes," he says, not caring whether it has or not.

"That must have been some fight. I wish I'd been there."

"Which one? I had three so far tonight. Won two."

"The one that messed up your face."

"That one was a draw. Right, Forge?" Ronnie turns to look into the back seat.

Forgione does not answer, and Ronnie stares at the face of the plump waitress who is receiving fully the fighter's plunging thrusts. Her head is pinned against the door of the car and bent forward, supported or obstructed as it is by the arm rest. Forgione's shoulder presses tightly into her chin, her eyes are shut lightly and her teeth clenched between parted—almost rolled back and sneering—lips. Her meaty fists clutch the shoulders of Forgione's short, zippered jacket; and her bare legs, as white in the radio light as Forgione's buttocks, are spread widely—one resting on the rear window shelf behind the back seat and the other, bent at the knee, dropped casually to the floor.

As Ronnie watches, her eyes open and roll up, then dart at Ronnie, quickly, almost in fright. Immediately, they shut again, squeezed tightly, as tightly as the fists clutching the jacket.

Ronnie feels a hand touch his chin, and turns as the blonde whispers: "Don't watch them."

He turns and drops slowly. Slowly. Falls slowly to her warm small breasts. Slowly far below. And this time she does not flinch as he kisses each of the hard nipples. Does not flinch as he draws one into his mouth. The palms of her hands hold his head, her fingers running deep into his long brown hair. And when he releases the wet breast and draws back to look at her in the radio light, he sees that she herself is now turned to watch with fascination the frantic action in the back seat that is rocking slightly, ever so slightly, the 1949 dark blue Ford in the rain on the road in the ice-crystal forest. And that her eyes are met with the vacant stare of those now open again on the face above Forgione's pinioning shoulder.

As Ronnie watches the distracted blonde in the radio light, he quietly slips his own sweater over his head and unbuttons his shirt. When his chest is exposed, he turns the girl toward himself and presses her naked flesh against his own. She relaxes luxuriously against him, her arms encircling his back under the open shirt as they kiss. But when Ronnie tries to lower her body on the seat, she suddenly tenses. "She won't put out," Forgione told him as they left the bar, whispering away from the girls, and Ronnie is now finding it to be true. Do what he will to her, she will not sprawl her delicate and thin body on the front seat beneath the yellow radio beams.

Now she and Ronnie are entangled fiercely upright, locked tightly against each other like two warring inter-twined snakes, wrestling for the big prize. Ronnie jams his mouth against hers, his tongue stabbing between her lips and tasting once again the blood from the puncture at the lower edge of his lower lip.

Now Ronnie's hand is far beneath her skirt, riding her thigh against the gentle grain of fuzz above her knees. Now the tips of his fingers close against the damp warmth of cloth that covers lightly and smoothly her prize. The legs open slowly as the tip of the middle finger presses the cloth into the soft orifice. The legs close on the hand, but the finger continues to work, forced on by the strain-ing muscles in Ronnie's wrist, forced against and into/against and into/against and into the increasing damp-ness of the cloth. Their kiss ends.

"You're hurting me," the girl whispers.

"Relax," Ronnie tells her.

Again, hesitantly, the legs part, close, part again. The

index finger hooks over the slippery, embroidered edge of the cloth, while the middle finger, trapping and uprooting hair, blunders its way, buries itself, and begins turning, squirming, pressing. At the same time, Ronnie's bloody lips press once more at the girl's mouth, into it; open as it is in the beginning of her ecstasy, around it opening with it, receive tongue, exchange tongues, through the taste of blood and mixed salivas, dead cigarette smoke and beer.

Now the finger withdraws and the legs move carefully, reluctantly together again. The four moist lips continue to slide against and into each other as Ronnie's hand works to the top edge of the underpants and begins to tug them down over the heart-shaped bulge of white hips. The girl's lips slide away from Ronnie's.

"No," she whispers, her mouth close to his ear. Her arms are under Ronnie's shirt, and she hooks her hands up over his shoulders to provide herself with the leverage to raise her body as Ronnie's hand pulls the underpants under her cold buttocks. She lifts one knee and draws her foot through, and the pants dangle now around her other knee. Ronnie's lips again swarm over her breasts, licking them, drawing them into his mouth, nipping at them with gentle teeth. She rests a hand lightly on his head as the lips move down to her flat expanse of stomach, and when the lips begin on the soft flesh of her inner thighs, she places another hand on the head, parting her legs to accept—and to encourage.

But as she awaits the touch of Ronnie's soft and swollen lips, she feels instead two rough fingers enter her, spreading and squirming deep inside, feels one penetrate her anus and the thumb roll and prod the hard button that rests above the squirming fingers. She feels lips—hundreds of lips—on her breasts again and on her neck biting and sucking, and a cry, a high-pitched grunt rises from her mouth, as a glow, a warm rocking hum starts in her thighs and mounts like a rush of liquid to her solar plexus. Ronnie's free arm now encircles the small of her back, bracing it against the driving work of the fingers and coaxing it along the seat so that she begins to slouch lower and lower, until at the last moment she raises her head that is about to slip from the edge of the seat and sees, standing white and upright in the radio light, the staff that Ronnie has erected somehow against the damp and cold night. "No," she gasps. "I can't. Don't make me. Oh." "She will not go down," Forgione tells him as they leave the bar, whispering away from the girls as the band behind them begins to dismantle amplifiers and speakers in the new bright light of the closing bar. The girl sits up quickly, dislodging Ronnie's fingers. To force her down again, Ronnie presses a kiss against her lips with as much weight as he can muster. But she will not budge, even though the fingers still squirm below, trying to regain lost ground. Ronnie takes her hand, the one that braces her against the seat, and folds it on himself, but she withdraws it immediately and whispers explosively in his ear: "They'll see." Together they turn to look into the back seat where Forgione's white buttocks continue to rise and fall above the fat waitress who now squeaks a short cry each time the big fighter's body descends. As before, her eyes are shut tightly. Ronnie impatiently draws back her hand and forces another kiss on the girl's reluctant lips. The hand recoils and he pulls it back again. When she rejects it a third time, he angrily withdraws his wet fingers from between her legs, and with both hands cupped behind her head, he begins to pull her down with an enraged strength. She struggles, but against her will she is pulled lower and lower until, turning her head aside at the last minute, Ronnie's erection slides along her powdered cheek and rubs against her ear. "Stop it," she screams, the noise piercing the drumming rain and soft radio music. The motion in the back seat pauses and then continues, and Ronnie releases the struggling head. The girl springs up and begins to fumble with the underpants dangling from one knee. She draws them up quickly, not bothering to twist them straight, and then aims a slap at Ronnie's face which he blocks easily, instinctively returning a punch of his own that catches her sharply on the mouth. A drop of blood swells on her lower lip, mixing with Ronnie's blood that is already smeared around her lip. She moves to the far side of the car and Ronnie moves after her, not to harm her, but to pull up on the door handle and swing the car door open, pushing her deftly and easily—since she is moving in that direction anyway—out onto the wet snowbank at the road's edge. "You son of a bitch!" she screams. Again the pumping in the back seat pauses. And Ronnie dumps her purse and coat out beside her and slams and locks the door.

He drives almost a mile before Forgione and the glassy-eyed waitress pop up in the back seat and ask in unison: "What happened?"

"We lost somebody," Ronnie answers quietly. He has lighted a cigarette from the blonde's pack which still sits on the dashboard above the radio.

"Are you going back for her?" Forgione asks.

"No," Ronnie says. He is driving too fast for the foggy, ice-covered road, and when the car drifts sideways on a shallow bend, Forgione says:

"Better slow down, Ron."

Ronnie decelerates and coughs on the cigarette smoke. The heads disappear, and in the rear-view mirror, Ronnie can see Forgione's white buttocks start up the pumping again.

From the floor Ronnie takes a can of beer that he and the blonde had been sharing. It feels empty, and when he lifts it to his lips, a few warm drops trickle into his mouth. They taste of ashes. Swinging the side vent open so that the chill rain blows on his face, he drops the can clunking on the road. Groping around on the wet floor, he finds the pack in which three cans remain. The car swerves, but he rights it and puts the beer on the seat beside him. With his cigarette in the corner of his mouth and his head cocked to keep the smoke out of his eyes, he wedges one of the cans between his legs and pulls the ring that opens it with a hiss. After he takes a gulp of the beer, he puts the can back between his legs and flips the radio dial across country music, pop music and commercials until he finds a news broadcast. The car now leaves the forest and comes into a small darkened town. A single red traffic light, swaying in the rain, flashes above the crossroads. The town looks familiar to Ronnie as he stops his car at the light. Facing him across the intersection is a gas station closed for the night, and on the opposite corner a general store that also houses the town's post office. There is a dim light in the back of this building, and Hank stands on the wooden front porch, knocking on the glass of the door; not as he did fifteen years ago, young and agile, but with his legs bowed and crippled from his motorcycle accident. An ancient crone comes to the door, wearing an apron and chewing a bite of her supper. Hank asks directions. Ronnie pulls into the cleared lot next to the building and stops beside a lighted telephone booth. He is disoriented. Is this the same town? Have they been parked out on the road near Timmons' cabin? He cannot be certain. The news ends, and Ronnie turns his attention to the sports announcer, who talks at some length about the main fight and then lists the results of the other fights in the auditorium. But it is only a list: "In the semifinal heavyweight Jack Forgione won a split decision over . . . In other bouts middleweight Ronnie

Man*der*ville knocked out . . ." When Forgione hears the names, he shouts: "That's us," and the pumping in the back seat continues rocking the car slightly on the icy, snow-packed lot. The winter's snow is packed deep on the lot. It has jammed open the door of the phone booth which stands a foot deep in the snow. During the day when the sun heats the glass sides of the booth, a foot of water accumulates in the booth, freezing again at night so that inside one stands level with the lot. But when Ronnie, hurrying through the rain to the booth, steps on this ice, it shatters and his foot sinks deep into the cold water. He curses and straddles the hole, bracing himself on the edges of the ice against the sides of the booth. A coin falls into the puddle between his legs as he fumbles a dime from the change in his pocket. Removing the receiver, he deposits this coin in the machine. Pushing the handful of change back into his pocket, he jams the humming receiver between his left ear and his shoulder and draws his wallet from his back pocket. He takes the slip of paper with the hospital number written on it, replaces the wallet and dials. The signal rings once and then is abruptly cut off as the dime drops down into the coin return chute. Ronnie retrieves it with his index finger and hears an operator say: "Deposit fifteen cents, please."

"Is this long distance?" Ronnie asks.

"Yes, sir," the operator answers. "Fifteen cents, please."

Ronnie puts the dime back in the slot and, forcing his hand into his tight pocket again, says: "I'll see if I can find a nickel."

He extracts the change and spreads it on the shelf in front of him. There are six pennies, three quarters and one dime.

"I don't have a nickel," he tells the operator.

"I'm sorry, sir, the charge is fifteen cents."

Using his right hand to brace and keep himself perched on the edges of the puddle, Ronnie swivels the upper half of his body to look for Forgione in the car. But he cannot see his friend or the waitress, and he does not want to interrupt them to ask for a nickel, so he faces the machine again and drops the other dime in the slot, hearing it ding twice as it drops.

"That is twenty cents, sir," the operator tells him.

"I couldn't find a nickel."

"It wasn't necessary to deposit twenty cents, sir. Perhaps you could get change somewhere."

Ronnie looks toward the dimly lit store. Hank is still standing on the porch tapping on the glass of the door. He turns slowly and grins at Ronnie, his missing teeth showing, blood running from both corners of his mouth.

"I can't get change," Ronnie shouts at her. "Do you know where this phone booth is?"

"You're in Cumberland County, sir."

"I'm in the puckerbush. That's where I am. The only living thing I can see is the trees and it's two o'clock in the morning . . ."

"Two thirty-six, sir."

"And you ask me to get change. Keep it. Keep the fucking nickel."

"If you'll give me your name and address, sir, the telephone company will be glad to send you a check for the amount of refund."

Ronnie is silent for a moment, and then he laughs very loudly against the cold night. The wind shifts for a moment and blows a gust of rain through the open door.

"I'd be ashamed to cash it," he says. " 'How would you like this, sir? One nickel or five pennies?' " Suddenly he shouts: "Please connect me, operator, or I'll come through this line and wring your neck."

"Thank you, sir," the operator says, and with a click the

open line is replaced by the buzz-buzz of the hospital number.

"Maine Medical," a woman's voice says suddenly.

"I'd like to find out the condition of a patient."

"Yes, sir."

"They told me to ask for the admitting department."

"Admitting is closed for the night, sir."

"How do I find out a patient's condition?"

"I have a list of recent admissions, sir."

"His name is Jacobs. Tony, I think, Jacobs."

"Are you a relative, sir?"

"No."

"I'm sorry, sir. But I cannot give you the information if you are not a relative."

Ronnie pauses. Hank is trying to turn away from the door of the store, but it is an arduous process since he must lift one bent leg at a time with his hands and turn it slightly and then lift the other and turn it and then the first, etc. His face shows the pain of the effort. Blood comes from his ears.

Ronnie softens his voice and with an exaggerated calmness says: "I am a relative. Sort of. In this way. I hit him in the jaw and he fell down and his head hit the canvas which is not supposed to hurt, so I guess what did it was when I hit him. And he wasn't feeling good so they took him to the hospital, but maybe you people let him go because he was conscious but throwing up. And then I called earlier and they told me to call back later and check. If he came there at all. He might be Catholic and couldn't come there anyway."

"Yes, I have that, sir. I was told you would call. Could you give me your name, please."

"Mandeville, Ronnie."

"Mr. Jacobs' condition is listed as fair, Mr. Mandeville."

"Oh," Ronnie says. Again the wind blows a spray of rain

through the doorway. Ronnie thinks for a moment and then says:

"What does that mean? Fair, I mean?"

"That's all I have listed, sir."

"Is he unconscious?"

"I couldn't say, sir. I imagine he is sleeping now."

"What does fair mean? Maybe, for all I know, he's fairly dead."

"No, sir. I have no critical listing for the patient."

"How can I find out? Can you connect me with a nurse on the floor?"

"No, sir. That is against hospital policy. I'm sure if you call back in the morning, after you get a good night's sleep, that the doctor's full report will be in and someone will be able to tell you more about the patient."

"Does fair mean he could be released tomorrow?"

"I wouldn't care to speculate, sir. I'm sure everything will be all right. If you have trouble sleeping, sometimes a cup of warm milk with a little butter melted into it will help. You call back in the morning. Everything's going to be all right now."

"Thank you."

"Good night, sir."

"Good night."

Forgione and the girl are sitting up as Ronnie slides back into the Ford.

"Who did you call?" Forgione asks.

"The hospital."

"How is he?"

"Fair."

"Oh," the big fighter says. The girl is tugging at him and he turns and kisses her. After a moment, he breaks it off and asks:

"What does that mean?"

"I don't know," Ronnie says, putting the car in gear and

driving away from Hank who is slowly approaching, the rain streaming down his bloody forehead.

Ronnie is a short way down the road when he remembers he has left the change and the hospital number on the shelf in the phone booth. He looks back toward the empty crossroads but Hank is shuffling under the flashing red light, moving in his direction through the icy rain.

"Let's go to my house and get something to eat," Forgione says.

"Naw, I'm still stuffed from those steaks," Ronnie says over his shoulder. "I want to keep on drinking."

"I got to eat something," Forgione tells him. "I'm starving."

"Me too," the waitress adds.

"Is there any beer left?" Forgione asks.

Ronnie passes the two remaining cans over the seat and hears them hiss as Forgione pulls their tops open.

On Route One Ronnie stops at an all-night diner and purchases a pack of cigarettes of the brand he smoked before he quit for his boxing. He also buys a dozen fresh doughnuts from the man who is frying them up for the morning and brings them out, hot and greasy in a brown paper bag, through the rain. Forgione and the waitress move into the front seat.

"Mm, good," Forgione says, biting into a warm doughnut. "How come you're smoking, Ron?"

"I don't know. I just wanted to," Ronnie tells him. "That girl left some in the car and I just started."

"Do you think we ought to go back and get her?" Forgione asks.

"Naw, she can call a cab or something when she gets to that phone booth."

"You better not do that to me," the waitress says.

"We will if you don't put out for my friend Ronnie,"

Forgione says, stuffing half a doughnut into her mouth.

"No problem," she says, chewing. "He's nice." She thrusts a hand, greasy from the doughnut it has been holding, between Ronnie's legs.

When Forgione goes into the diner to buy a morning paper, she lets Ronnie squeeze her mammoth breasts, but Ronnie has lost his mood for it, and by the time Forgione returns to the car, he is smoking another cigarette and finishing the waitress' can of beer.

With the dim interior light on, Forgione reads aloud the short accounts of their fights as they drive. They are not far from the Mandeville farm, but by the time they arrive, they have finished all the beer and doughnuts.

"I'll get us some whiskey," Ronnie tells them, turning off the car's light and letting it drift to a halt before it reaches the driveway. "There's plenty left from the party today. I'll be right out."

He gets out of the car and whistles softly for the dog, who comes to greet him wagging its tail. As he walks up the driveway with the dog jumping beside him, he sees that the kitchen light is still on and that Boyd's station wagon is parked near the porch. Large wet flakes of snow are now falling with the rain. Ronnie's jacket is soaked through and he wants to change it if he can get to his room unnoticed. He had counted on Virginia Jane's being asleep. What time is it? Three? Three-thirty? The saturated shoe and sock squeak on the ice of the driveway. He remembers that Grandpa Simmons is there too; but he knows the old man will be dead asleep with all the liquor he poured into himself. But what about Boyd?

Like an Indian scout, like THE Indian Scout, the masked man's faithful Indian companion, Ronnie treads softly up the edge of the porch steps. The faithful Indian companion used to do this, of course, on the back stairs of frontier hotels, knowing full well, of course of course, it makes so much sense, that the center of each step might creak, even from the weight of a sneaky Indian. Ronnie totters, catches Him-Sneaky-Self—he might be just a little drunk—and crosses the porch which creaks. How would the faithful Indian deal with this porch? Walk around the edge of course of course. But the jumping running tail-wagging dog is making so much noise that it doesn't matter. And the rain is drumming on the porch roof. And Boyd is sitting at the kitchen table—big fucking cowpoke—drinking a glass of milk (sarsaparilla?) and reading. Ronnie squints. His long hair leaks rain into his eyes. The Bible!

Ronnie bends to quiet the dog, but when he stings it with his finger on the end of the nose, it begins to bark. Suddenly Boyd is at the door. The Indian flattens himself against the wall of the house. If he is discovered, he will be forced to try to take this white cowpoke's scalp, Bible or no Bible, and he has tried that once this evening and doesn't want to try again. The knife is clenched tightly between his teeth. The steel is cold.

The glint in his eye is cold.

The dog darts to Ronnie, nudges his leg once, and then runs into the house as Boyd holds the door open. When the door slams shut, Ronnie pivots quickly to the window, and sure enough! The big cowboy has a mouse the size of a tangerine, all purple and rust, swelling shut his left eye.

Ronnie smiles. Boyd sits at the table and scratches the dog's head. But the dog won't sit still. It rushes to the door. And back to Boyd and to the door and back to Boyd, who now ignores it, turning back—Ronnie smiles again—to the word of the Lord, which he must cock his head to read through his only functioning eye.

Virginia Jane comes into the kitchen, and Boyd turns his good eye to her as she sits at the table facing the window. Ronnie backs away from the light to the far edge of the porch. He cannot see the kitchen clock, and he cannot remember when he has ever seen his mother up at this hour. And why is Boyd there? Virginia Jane seems to be crying, but it is hard to tell. Perhaps she is only tired. She leans her head forward, propping it on the heels of her palms. To comfort her, Boyd gets up and stands behind her massaging her back and shoulders. She touches one of his hands. Thank you. You're such a comfort. One of the hands drops; begins to massage a breast. She covers the hand with her own hand. A blouse button is undone. The hand moves inside; climbs the rim of her bra; snuggles inside. Another button is undone, and the blouse is spread open.

Ronnie is running wildly down the driveway, slipping and sliding. There is no more rain, only large wet flakes on the snow and ice. Large wet flakes of snow large wet flakes large wet flakes. Zzzzzzz. Ronnie dashes headlong through the front door of the house, bounding up the front stairs to his room. Ronnie slips quietly through the front door, easing it shut behind him. There is a slight click as the door shuts, but in the kitchen they seem not to have heard it. Someone drives up. He is afraid for a moment that it is Forgione, but the keys to the Ford are in his own pocket so it couldn't be.

The bottles of liquor are still on the buffet in the darkened living room. Ronnie takes a half-full bottle of Scotch, and then begins his soft tread up the edges of the front stairs. He hears a car door slam and imagines Virginia Jane hastily buttoning her blouse, touching her hair, drying her eyes, standing up, striding to the side door.

The light is on in the upstairs hallway, and Ronnie moves quickly to his room. The only noise is the slight squooshing of his right shoe.

In his room, Ronnie pushes the door shut and snaps on the ceiling light. Will someone outside see? Will someone, happening into the dark cold living room below, notice the light from above reflected on the field of snow? The bed moans, and Ronnie snaps the switch off, catching a glimpse of Grandpa Simmons, now wearing a pair of Ronnie's pajamas—where did she find those?—and tucked neatly into Ronnie's bed. The old man's expensive gray suit is neatly laid out on the chair beside the bed. Ronnie freezes at the light switch, making sure that the old man is still asleep. Then he gropes his way toward the closet in search of a dry jacket, gripping his bottle by the neck. He lurches and his forehead collides sharply with the open edge of the closet door. Whispering curses, he feels his way inside the closet, wading through the tangle of laundry on the floor. His open hand is searching the dark wall when he hears people coming up the back stairs. He manages to pull the closet door shut before they enter the room. The room light goes on, and Ronnie can see the thin line of it at the bottom of the closet door. His feet are hopelessly trapped, twisted across each other as he faces the door, bracing himself against the wall with his free hand. Nothing to do but sit down cross-legged, campfire style, easily, the Indian scout making no noise whatsoever, the Scotch now cradled in his lap.

"I didn't realize I had shut the door to the room," he hears Virginia Jane say.

"Maybe I did it," Boyd says. They seem to be near the bed.

"How did you expect me to hear him if he called?" Virginia Jane snaps.

But now there is a third voice, a man. "Has he been conscious?"

"Some," Virginia Jane answers. "At least he talked to us. It wasn't too coherent."

"Does he have any heart history?"

"Not that I know of." There is a silence. The darkness

becomes oppressive around Ronnie. Without a target for him to focus on, he becomes dizzy. He shuts his eyes but that only makes it worse. He uncorks the bottle and sips from it, and begins to grope silently on the floor around him for a dry sock.

"I thought he was just tired," Virginia Jane says. "He came up from Florida for the funeral. It took several days by bus." She talks fast, panicked, running on. "I thought he was just tired and had too much to drink. I didn't realize he was sick, or I would have called you earlier. I'm sorry to make you come out at such an hour in this weather. My God, what a night."

The doctor does not answer her. Apparently he is working over the gray old man in Ronnie's bed. Ronnie imagines stethoscope, pulse checks, thermometers; Virginia Jane hovering, wringing her hands; Boyd standing to one side, put in his place, his hands folded responsibly behind his back, Pa-RADE rest. Pensive, alert, sympathetic, Christian, loving, loyal, trustworthy, kind, true, brave.

Ronnie locates a sock, and placing it in his lap, begins to remove his wet shoe. This is a difficult task on the dark floor. The shoe squeaks when Ronnie draws it over his heel, and when he has peeled the wet sock away, he begins to tremble in the naked air. Again he drinks from the Scotch bottle, a long gulp that convulses him in silent gagging. He gets the urge to light a cigarette, but he knows the smoke will give him away.

No one in the room has spoken, but now footsteps are moving across the creaking boards of the floor in the direction of the closet. Ronnie freezes, one hand touching the pack of cigarettes in his pocket and the other about to cork the bottle wedged between his legs. The footsteps stop. Ronnie looks up to the level of the faces he expects to see when the door is thrown open.

"Please don't be alarmed by what I'm about to say."

It is the doctor's voice, low and calm, just outside the closet where he has drawn them away from the patient. "There is no cause for alarm, but there has been a serious strain on his heart." The doctor pauses, apparently waiting for a reaction. He continues: "Not an arrest, but a strain. I emphasize that. His beat is fairly regular now."

Virginia Jane interrupts. "Is there permanent damage?" Her voice is calm and clinical, as if she is talking about a car. Yes, permanent damage to the frame, which is why we can't align the wheels properly.

"I can't determine that here. But, I'd say that chances are there's nothing a good rest wouldn't cure. I'd like to have him in the hospital for several days where we can watch him and run some tests on him."

"Do you want him to go to the hospital now?" Virginia Jane asks.

"Yes. As soon as possible."

"What is it? What's the problem?" Grandpa Simmons is suddenly bellowing from the bed. "Who's there? Ginny. Is that you?"

"Yes, Papa. It's all right. The doctor is here."

The old man does not answer. Apparently he has fallen asleep again, or perhaps it is too much of an effort for him to say more.

"How will we get him there?" Virginia Jane whispers.

"My station wagon is rigged as an ambulance for the volunteer fire department," Boyd says. "It just takes a minute to set it up."

The boards creak as they begin to move away from the closet door. The doctor adds: "You don't have to go along, Virginia. You can visit tomorrow. There's nothing to worry about."

"I want to," she says.

"One more thing," the doctor says. "Could you wake Ronnie, so he can help us carry Mr. Simmons."

"Ronnie?" Virginia Jane asks. Ronnie corks the bottle. His mother's voice sounds confused. "Ronnie . . . ah . . . Ronnie left. He's not here."

"I saw his car," the doctor says. Ronnie freezes again, his hand still on the bottle. "It was parked out on the road when I drove in."

"Oh, no," Virginia Jane moans. Ronnie pictures her holding her forehead, stumbling; Boyd supporting her.

"Was there anyone in it?" Boyd asks.

"I didn't see anyone."

Ronnie wonders for a second where Forgione and the waitress are, but he knows almost instantly that they are again on the back seat, no heads visible, rocking. Ronnie, himself, begins to rock in his cross-legged position; rocking forward and back, forward and back, to ease the tension. Again he uncorks the bottle.

"He's here somewhere," Virginia Jane whines. "Oh no. He's outside watching. Maybe he's even in the house. He's the cause of everything. He got Papa all worked up, he hit Mr. Boyd and had a fight with Bunnie's boy friend."

"It'll be all right, Virginia," Boyd says. Ronnie imagines him draping his big arm over her shoulders, diminishing them, swallowing them.

"It won't be all right." Her voice rises. "He's crazy."

Ronnie's rocking ceases.

"You're damn right," Grandpa Simmons shouts suddenly. "He's crazy."

"I think he'll settle down," Boyd says. "He's a good boy. He's upset because of his father's accident."

"He should be upset," Virginia Jane screams. "He was there when it happened."

There it is. The accusation, finally. And Ronnie can only sit frozen in mid-rock, leaning forward, the uncorked bottle in his hands. What does she mean? Does she think he was in the loft? He was there when it happened.

There? Where? He wants to shake her and scream at her. Where? WHERE?

Where do you think I was? I was out in the yard. Out in the yard. Out in the yard.

I heard Bunnie scream, and I ran into the barn and there he was. Bunnie was first. Ask her if I was there. Go ahead, ask her.

"Please," the doctor says firmly, slightly angry. "This is not helping the patient."

"Goddamn crazy. Just like his father," Grandpa Simmons shouts.

Then they are gone: Boyd carrying the tiny old man down the back stairs like a new bride, and Virginia Jane turning off the room light behind them. Ronnie is not sure they are gone. He sits quietly in the closet, waiting to hear the side door shut, and draws on the dry warm sock he has found in the tangled pile of laundry. He struggles into his wet shoe and ties it in the darkness. When he hears the door downstairs, he comes out of the closet and stands near the cold window watching Boyd put Grandpa Simmons on the cot in the back of his station wagon. Virginia Jane looks around the yard suspiciously—I'm up here, Mom—and then climbs in beside her father. The doctor's car follows the station wagon out of the driveway, both cars rolling through the new snow that muffles the sound of their engines.

When they are gone, the room seems comfortable to Ronnie. He feels no need to leave, to rush away. Instead, he sits on the edge of his bed and lights a cigarette. The hall light coming through the door illuminates the curling smoke. How odd the cigarette looks to him, wedged between his fingers. He draws smoke from it, inhales successfully, stifling the swelling protest in his lungs, and blows the smoke at the light. A warmth comes over his body and relaxes him, and he lies back on the bed studying the pattern of ceiling cracks, almost too dimly lit for him to see but familiar to his memory. It is impossible for him to think of Hank as dead, the abruptness of that death delaying the reality of it for him. His comfort is complete on the soft bed. It surges warmly through him. He knows he must not fall asleep with the lighted cigarette in his hand. The warmth extends to Hank. Ronnie misses him in a sentimental way. He wants to see him again, to say something to make him laugh, to share the bottle of Scotch that is resting beside him on the bed. But a sudden vision of Hank inside the closed coffin makes him uneasy: the gray face, the peaceful eyelids, the large bruises showing through the make-up, and the black surface of the inner lid of the coffin.

Ronnie sits up quickly when the cigarette burns his finger. Swearing, he throws the butt on the floor and tramps on it. He sees his socks then, the new one white and the older one gray. The new sock had looked gray when he held it near the light coming under the closet door. He laughs aloud at himself.

And only when his laughing in an empty room makes him look up self-consciously does he see the hulking silhouette of the man standing in the bedroom doorway.

The short burst of breath that explodes from Ronnie is a gasp, a choked scream. Hank has come to kill him. HANK KILLS MEN. Ronnie reaches for the Scotch bottle to use as a club, but the bottle slips from his grasp and clunks to the floor. Ronnie cannot stand up. It's too late. He's been caught. There is nothing he can do; nothing he could ever do.

"I didn't mean to scare you," Forgione says. "Christ, you jumped about a mile."

"I was thinking about something."

"What the hell were you laughing about? You're crazy as a loon."

"Look at my socks," Ronnie says, retrieving the bottle from the floor.

Forgione looks and laughs. "How did that happen?" he asks.

"It's a long story," Ronnie tells him.

"Come on. Are you going?"

"Sure," Ronnie says. He does not move.

"You took the keys and we got cold as hell out there. Then I saw two cars drive out, and I thought maybe you left or something. So I came looking for you."

"Have a drink," Ronnie says, offering the bottle. Forgione takes it and drinks.

"If you want to stay home, I can take your car and bring it back tomorrow." Forgione wipes his lips and returns the bottle to him.

"No. I can't stay here. They didn't even know I came in. I hid. I want to get the hell out of here."

"Well, let's go."

"O.K., sure." He does not move.

"Well?"

Ronnie fumbles in his pocket and extracts the car keys. "Here," he says. "Take these and turn the heater on. I'll be out in a minute. I want to get some more of my stuff."

Forgione takes the keys and turns to leave.

"Get a couple of bottles of the whiskey that's down in the dining room," Ronnie says.

"Hurry up," Forgione says over his shoulder as he descends the back stairs.

"I'll be right out," Ronnie tells him.

Ronnie lights another cigarette after Forgione has gone. He remains on the edge of the bed, but after several meditative puffs, he crushes the cigarette on the floor and stands up and walks out into the hall.

He is not able to decide which way to go once he is in the hallway. He looks down the back stairs. There is no light in the kitchen and the stairs dissolve into darkness. He turns and walks instead down the hallway, slowly, unsteadily, tottering once and clunking the bottle that dangles from his hand against the wall.

Near the front stairs, the door to Bunnie's room is ajar, and Ronnie stops beside it. He does not turn to face it, but instead looks down the curving front stairs which also lead into the darkness below. He starts hesitantly forward and then stops again. The door opens slowly as he pushes it, and before the light from the hall falls across his sister's face, he slips into her room. Bunnie is sleeping curled on her side, and Ronnie crouches beside the bed, facing her. He moves close enough to her lips to smell tobacco smoke on her sleepy breath. A strand of hair curls beside Bunnie's ear. Ronnie touches this and feels the flushed heat of sleep on the cheek beneath it. He straightens up and sits on the edge of the bed with his back to his sister. Bunnie shifts slightly and flops an arm beside him, and as Ronnie uncorks the Scotch bottle and drinks from it, he strokes the arm.

When he has corked the bottle and placed it on the floor beside the bed, Ronnie kneels and touches his lips to the soft flesh inside the elbow of this arm. Here too is the welcoming hotness. He runs his finger over her lips, open and thick with sensuous night-time breathing. He bends to kiss her, but when his lips block this breathing, Bunnie's head moves away, and she turns, flopping on her back with her arm touching Ronnie's side. Ronnie tugs at the crotch of his pants to straighten the erection that has grown there, and then on an impulse, he unzips the pants and frees it to stand thick and tall, swaying ponderously in the light from the hallway.

The covers move easily down Bunnie's thin body, and when they are at her waist, Ronnie bends and kisses each of her breasts through the flannel nightgown she is wearing. He squeezes the flanneled nipples with his lips, and then slides the covers down to Bunnie's ankles. The nightgown has bunched up at Bunnie's hips, exposing her long thin legs, and Ronnie kisses each hot thigh while using only his thumb to carefully slide up the folds of flannel as he kneels between the flatly reclining legs. Suspending his body over hers with one stiff arm, Ronnie uses his free hand to guide himself to her, so that when it finds the opening it seeks, it is the only part of his body that touches her. Bunnie's sleeping body begins to respond to Ronnie's firm and insistent pressure, but she is dry and Ronnie must wait at the entrance, following his sister's body as it squirms about the bed, until her juices begin to flow and he slides easily—more easily than he had anticipated—deep inside her.

Frightened now, almost reconsidering, Ronnie holds himself above her, his heart thumping wildly. When he is sure she has not awakened, he pulls back and plunges deeply again; the breath that he has held too long exploding from him almost simultaneously with her first screams.

Perhaps he could stay. Lock himself there. Really, what could she do at this point? But Bunnie's first panicked and instinctive heave, with her scream piercing the back of his head and bringing on the sharp pains of earlier in the evening, rolls him heavily to the floor. The Scotch bottle breaks. Ronnie bounds up. He still has some idea that she will not know who he is. And through the door. Anonymous? He leaps down into the darkness of the stairs, zipping his pants as he runs, and slams the front door on the continuing shrieks coming from his sister's bedroom.

# VII

Ronnie slides behind the wheel and pulls the car into the driveway, braking it hastily and reversing it out onto the light snow cover of the road again, this time facing toward the town.

"Where are we going?" Forgione asks. His voice is muffled against the cheek of the waitress.

"Ride around. Drink," Ronnie tells him, addressing the rear-view mirror.

"I'm pretty drunk," Forgione replies.

"I know," says the waitress. Her voice sounds far away, small.

"Did you get some of those bottles?" Ronnie asks.

"Two," Forgione says. "They're both half full. I've got them back here."

"Give me one," Ronnie tells him. Without looking back, he puts his hand over the seat.

The road is littered with branches and twigs broken by the weight of the ice, and several times before he reaches town, Ronnie must guide the car around large fallen limbs. A news broadcast bleeps and crackles on the car radio, and Ronnie quickly flips across the dial to country music. He takes a long swallow from the bottle, gagging loudly, and his shoulders convulse in a shudder.

The town is dark and empty. Yesterday's snow is piled in rainy lumps at the edges of the sidewalks. The new snow has smoothed the edges of these lumps and is starting to blend into them. A single yellow light bulb dangles above Boyd's desk in the gas station. The fisherman's restaurant is closed. No sound comes from the dark harbor.

"Do you want us to sit up front?" Forgione asks.

"Sure," Ronnie says. "I'll stop in a minute."

They drive out of town on the ocean road, heading toward the cemetery. Ronnie turns carefully into the slick cemetery drive, and although he sees the heavy chain suspended between the stone gateposts, the snow-covered ice will not hold his brake-locked front wheels. The car slides gently into the chain; there is a crunching sound, the tinkling of broken glass, and suddenly the cemetery ahead of them goes dark in the snowfall and they are stopped with the dull vibration of the ocean pounding the rocks somewhere below them. On the radio, the twang of a guitar needles the silence of the stalled motor.

Ronnie says: "Fuck," and steps from the car into the darkness, slamming the door angrily. Forgione also gets out, and together they inspect the damage. The waitress watches them behind the slap-slap, slap-slap sound of the windshield wipers.

Only the headlights are damaged. These are shattered, jammed against the taut chain. Bracing his arm on a fender of the car, Ronnie bends to inspect the grillwork, which is intact.

Forgione stands over him, his arms folded for warmth. "Why did you turn in here?" he asks. "This is the cemetery."

Without looking up at him, Ronnie whispers: "I wanted to fuck your friend."

"Oh," Forgione says, and then adds rhetorically: "She said it was all right sort of, didn't she?"

"Yes," Ronnie says, standing up.

"You want me to go for a walk or something?" Forgione asks.

"It would make it easier for me."

"Lemme get a bottle," Forgione says.

"Shut off the ignition," Ronnie tells him.

Forgione walks back and opens the car door. The windshield wiper and radio noise stop when he takes the keys from the ignition. "Me and Ronnie are going for a little walk," he tells the girl, who then glances out at Ronnie. "He'll be back in a few minutes. I'll be back in about half an hour." He slams the door and returns with the bottle and whispers to Ronnie: "Walk a little way with me, and then you can come back."

They duck under the chain and start down the icy cemetery road, walking unsteadily. Forgione opens the bottle and drinks from it.

"What are you going to do about headlights?" he asks Ronnie, passing him the bottle.

"I got the key to a gas station in town where I can get some new ones," Ronnie says. He drinks and shudders.

They walk on in the dark snowfall. The boom of the ocean surrounds them. Ronnie lights a cigarette. He has not changed his rain-soaked jacket and he begins to tremble in the cold.

When they reach the site for Hank's grave, Ronnie stops and says: "Here's where they buried my dad."

"Where? Right here?" Forgione turns to him, astonished. "You mean this is the same cemetery? Today?"

"Yes. But they didn't bury him exactly." He offers Forgione the bottle, but the big fighter declines, preferring to keep his cold hands jammed in his pockets. "They don't bury him until the ground thaws," Ronnie continues. "I think the casket is over there in that shed." He points with the bottle to the outline of the tool shed in the far corner of the white cemetery.

"Oh," Forgione says. He looks at the ground in embarrassment. "I don't think they do that in Portland any more. They probably use a jackhammer or something to dig through the frost."

"Yes," Ronnie says. "It seems kind of old-fashioned." He too is looking uncomfortably at his feet, and he adds: "Your uncle digs foundations now in the winter, doesn't he?"

"It depends on how much money is involved, you know, on loans and time limits and stuff. They have special equipment too."

"How deep is it frozen?"

"I don't know. Maybe eighteen inches of frost, I think. Or three feet."

They both fall silent, facing each other. Ronnie, the drunker of the two, sways slightly, the bottle dangling from his hand.

"I wonder if he's in that tool shed?" Ronnie says softly to the ground beneath him.

"What?" Forgione asks, looking up.

"Nothing. I'm going to check on something. Here." He thrusts the bottle suddenly at Forgione and dashes off toward the tool shed. Forgione, bewildered, watches him run, glancing back several times in the direction of the car.

Ronnie slips once on the icy road and sprawls in the snow. He is up quickly, however, brushing his clothes as he runs. Trotting up to the tool shed, he raises his foot and stomps open the padlocked wooden door. The door crashes against the inside wall of the shed, and Ronnie's momentum carries him inside the small building and drops him to his knees on the rough board floor.

Puffing, he continues to kneel while he takes a pack of matches from his pockets and lights one. In the flaring light he sees that there are no coffins in the shed; only gardening and lawn-cutting tools, picks and shovels for gravedigging.

When Ronnie returns carrying two picks and a shovel, Forgione is seated on the edge of a gravestone, swilling from the bottle of whiskey. He looks at the equipment and then at Ronnie and says flatly: "No." He stands the whiskey bottle upright in the snow and begins to giggle.

"Do what you want," Ronnie tells him. He drops the two picks and begins to shovel excess snow away from the plot that will eventually serve as Hank's grave.

"Wouldn't you rather climb into a nice warm waitress?" Forgione asks, snickering. "I'm telling you she may be fat, but she really knows how to use it. She's got these little muscles in her cunt that milk you dry. You ought to try." He giggles at his rhyme and says: "And anything is better than digging a hole in a cemetery in a blizzard."

"Do what you want," Ronnie repeats. "You don't have to sit there and watch if you don't want to. Take the car and go home." He finishes clearing the snow away and flings the shovel aside.

"No headlights," Forgione reminds him. He lifts the bottle out of the snow and drinks from it.

"You don't have to stick around," Ronnie says. He takes up a pick and swings it angrily at the ground. The point glances off the ice and twists the heavy tool out of his hands.

Forgione puts the bottle down and retrieves the pick. "If I didn't stay with you tonight, you would kill yourself." Forgione is still smiling. "Your cowboy friend would have pounded you into the sidewalk if I wasn't there, and Angelo would have beat you so hard with his billy club you'd be weaving baskets at the state hospital for the rest of your life." He pushes Ronnie away from the grave site. "A pick is a dangerous tool in the hands of an amateur," he says, gripping the handle. "You can put it through your shin just as easily as you can put it through the ground. But what you want to do"—he swings down heavily and drives the pick several inches through the ice —"is keep it going straight into the ground. And then lift." A chunk of ice and dirt crumble away when he lifts the tool. "Now, how much of this do you want to dig up?"

Ronnie bends down for the whiskey bottle. "Well, just a foot or two so they have to finish it and bury him."

"One foot or two feet?" Forgione asks.

"Two feet and make it straight."

"O.K., but you stay at your end. That pick could go through my skull just as easy it could go through your shin."

They both take up picks and begin to work earnestly at the frozen earth. The snowfall grows lighter and the air colder, but neither notices. They swing their tools alternately, and after about fifteen minutes of this rhythmic chopping they have crumbled away a rectangular section of the surface that is the size of a grave. Both are sweating freely. Forgione takes up the shovel to clear the crumbled earth and ice away from the section, and Ronnie steps back to inspect their work.

"Your uncle should dig graves instead of building houses," Ronnie says, wiping his brow with the sleeve of his damp jacket. Forgione grunts, tossing clods over on another grave, and Ronnie adds: "Then he could paint on all his trucks: 'Our houses last till doomsday.' "

Forgione steps out of the shallow pit, and Ronnie says: "Hand me the liquor."

They both drink, and Forgione sits on an adjoining gravestone. Altogether, taking turns digging and drinking, they are able to chip out approximately two feet of frozen dirt in about an hour. The snow stops, and as the sky clears, the horizon over the ocean lightens quickly. Their work stops when Forgione begins to vomit.

"That's enough," he says, retching over the stone on which he has been sitting. "That's absolutely enough." He stands up when he is finished and smashes the nearly empty bottle on the gravestone and begins to stumble up the road to the car.

"I'll be up in a minute," Ronnie says, puffing and leaning on his pick. But almost as soon as Forgione leaves, he turns and walks in the opposite direction, carrying the pick slung over his shoulder like a rifle. He passes the tool shed, and continues to walk with determination as the road turns toward the far corner of the cemetery. In this corner, overlooking the ocean, sits the cemetery's only mausoleum, belonging to the town's most prominent family. This is the only other structure in the cemetery in which coffins could be stored.

Ronnie can see the gray ocean as he stands before the tomb. The wind has increased, and as far as he can see under the clearing sky, whitecaps swell up and disappear on the rough water. The tomb is a squat granite structure. The name PERKINS is chiseled in a marble lintel above the green bronze-plated door. A small seraph in a flowing robe and a cherub with caricatured chubby cheeks rest on inset shelves on either side of the door.

Holding the door shut is a heavy padlock which breaks easily when Ronnie strikes down on it with the pick. Flipping the latch away, he pushes the wide door but can move it only slightly. By leaning his shoulder against it he is able to push it open slowly. When the door is open, he steps back in the snow but the light is still too dim to enable him to see inside the tomb. Squinting, he steps inside and leans his pick against the wall. There is no identifiable smell, but the frozen dankness is somehow familiar to Ronnie. He is sure Hank is here, and his heart quickens as he fumbles for the pack of matches in his pocket.

In the fast first light of the match, he sees five coffins on shelves lining the sides of the small room. One coffin is small, half-sized, and Ronnie first thinks of a midget, but when he strikes the second match, he realizes that this is a child's coffin. The brass plate on this shelf reads "Russell Remick Perkins, a loving son, May 3, 1931–February 22, 1932." Ronnie does not read the other plates. All the coffins have ornate carvings in metal or wood; none are Hank's. He lights a third match and sees that he is standing on a dirt floor. Near his feet is the white skull of a small animal, a rat, a mouse or a snake. There are bunches of dried or frozen, rotting flowers on the floor and on some of the coffins, and in the left corner on a shelf stands an elaborate gold cross. The wind blows across the open door behind him and when he turns, it is lighter outside, and he can see across the entire white field of the cemetery. Ice coats each of the hundreds of gray monument stones, and he can see the exposed earth of the hole he and Forgione have dug. The dark hulk of the Ford is pressed against the entrance chain.

Ronnie leaves the tomb, ignoring the pick leaning against the wall. With his hands in his pockets, he walks slowly back to the car. He pauses to stare at the shallow pit he has just dug. The wind pushes at him, and after several seconds, he walks briskly to the car, trotting the last few steps and flinging the door open.

Forgione and the waitress lie huddled together on the back seat. Their eyes are closed, and their arms are tucked at odd angles in the cramped space. Ronnie assumes they are asleep, but when he slams the door, Forgione says softly:

"What were you doing in that tomb, Ron?"

"Trying to find something to put in our hole," Ronnie tells him, starting the car.

"A coffin?" Forgione asks, but his question is unconcerned in his half-sleep, and Ronnie does not answer him.

The Ford's muffler rumbles and crackles as Ronnie backs the car out of the cemetery drive. A red glow has appeared above the horizon, and it is now light enough to drive without headlights.

As Ronnie turns onto the main street, he sees the familiar trucks of the fishermen parked on both sides of the street near the restaurant. Gusts of wind spin snow along the curbs. The car heater has not yet overtaken the chill inside the car, and Ronnie begins to tremble. Jamming the whiskey bottle between his legs, he uncaps it and raises it to his lips as he passes the restaurant. Although it is now almost full dawn, Boyd's gas station is closed. The lot around the pumps and garage doors has not been plowed, and Ronnie can see no tire tracks in the fresh snow.

When he reaches the end of the town's small business section, he drives straight ahead on a road that leads eventually to another small town several miles down the coast. Through the sparkling ice-covered trees Ronnie can see bursts of the sun rising large and low over the ocean. The violent wind shatters ice from branches above the car and the fragments shower down over the roof and windshield.

Ronnie does not pull the car onto the semicircular drive of the Stevens Funeral Home. Instead, he parks it on the road, jammed against a snow bank, partially hidden by the bushes and alders of the field next door. Before he opens the car door, he takes another long swallow of whiskey and slides the closed bottle under the front seat. Stepping out onto the shining white road, he shuts the door gently so he will not waken Forgione and the waitress who slumber together in the back seat.

The house is a large three-story structure with gingerbread trim, a captain's walk around the roof, and a cupola complete with look-out post and clock facing the sea. The front yard looks down on a long, sloping hill leading to a vast marsh meadow that ends in a line of sand dunes, a beach and the ocean.

In this light, the shadow of the house seems to stretch all the way to the woods behind it. Ice-covered bushes at both ends of the driveway vibrate in the buffeting wind and cast long shadows across the waist-deep snow of the yard. Ronnie hides momentarily behind one of these bare bushes and then dashes up the driveway, racing at his own shadow as he runs. When he is under the car portico at the front of the house, he pauses to catch his breath before climbing the steps to the front porch.

The boards creak as Ronnie tries the six windows, none of which he can raise. When he has tried them all, he turns the knob of the heavy front door. It swings open silently, and he steps into the warm and flowery entrance hall.

Ronnie begins to tremble. He feels hot and nauseous; and the smell of death, of flowers and rot, the same smell he has lived with for three days in his own house, overwhelms him. Red and green and golden light falls through the door transom, and Ronnie's eyes, still blinded from sunlight on snow, see little else in the dim hall. There are wide doorways leading to the two front rooms on either side of the hall, but both are blocked by folding screens. Ronnie moves quickly—as he must—to stifle his impulse to vomit, darting behind the screen on his left and into an empty, brightly sunlit room. Through the long window Ronnie sees his own footprints in the snow on the porch. He has tracked snow on the red carpet of this empty room. The snow is melting. The room is empty but untidy. Beige and gray metal folding chairs line three walls. Wilted flower petals, dried stems, bits of tissue paper clutter the floor. The dark cloth that covers the oblong coffin platform at the end of the room opposite the windows is ripped, showing plywood beneath it.

Ronnie rushes from the room. He is dizzy and must keep moving. He bumps the screen but catches it and rights it with an awkward struggle. He sees a large potted plant now by the front door. He ducks behind the other screen and into a dark flower-stuffed room. Heavy drapes block the windows, and the only light in the room comes through the church-like transoms. The room is arranged like the one across the hall. Except the rug is clean; or looks clean in the red and yellow light. Except the room is half-filled with baskets and displays of flowers and their warm overwhelming odor. Except the coffin platform at the far end of the room holds a coffin. Except the room smells of the rankness of death. And the coffin is closed.

Ronnie faces the coffin. His dizziness has passed and he begins to sweat. He knows that Hank lies inside. As he stands before the coffin, he pictures the way Hank looks in repose. His sideburns have been shaved and his crewcut shortened. His face is gray and caked with make-up.

The handle is directly in front of him, but he cannot bring himself to lift the lid. His eyes have not adjusted to the dim light. Abruptly he walks away from the bier, walks around the room. He examines the tags on the displays of flowers without really reading them or taking note of the names. He walks to the door of the room and looks out into the hallway, cocking his head to listen for sounds in the sleeping, dawn-struck house. There is silence, except for the whistle of the wind and the dry bushes beating against the clapboards. He hears the furnace come on with a muffled roar in the basement, and he turns back into the room. Again he stands before the coffin, and again he cannot bring himself to touch it. He wipes at the sweat on his forehead with the back of his hand. He begins to feel dizzy again, so he grabs suddenly at the lid handle and lifts. In the first instant of his action, he notices that the coffin is somewhat fancier than the one Hank was in, but he continues to push the lid up quickly until it bounces against the wall behind it. The old lady at rest on the white satin startles him. He had expected Hank, and finding Miss Something-or-other—he cannot remember her name—a teacher at the town elementary school, is a surprise.

When he begins to pull the old lady from her resting place, her white hair becomes disheveled. Her head is jammed against his stomach, forcing her frameless glasses at an awkward angle over her nose. The lid teeters from Ronnie's effort and then falls heavily across the lady's thin chest. The head comes loose, and Ronnie topples backwards with it in his hands. He drops it before he hits the ground and it comes to rest on its side, facing away from him. There is something wet on Ronnie's hands, and he wipes them furiously on his pants as he scrambles to his feet and dashes from the room.

In the hallway he vomits into the potted palm, dropping

to his knees and retching countless times into the sandy soil.

There are other rooms and doorways at the back of the hall. A large sitting room has comfortable furniture and an open fireplace with an ornate cast-iron front surrounding it. Two doors open into coat closets and a third hides cleaning supplies and equipment: vacuum, bucket, mop, floor wax, rags, furniture polish, feather duster and the smell of disinfectant. A swinging door at the end of the hall leads into a bare white storage room. Several empty glass vases sit on the drainboard of a double sink. The drawers and cabinets around the walls of the kitchen echo the room's emptiness as Ronnie opens and bangs them shut. In the cabinets he finds more of the plain glass vases, and in the drawers, piles of ribbons and bows, and various somber drop cloths of black or dark reds or blues. The liquid is still on Ronnie's hands, sticky and sweet-smelling. He takes handfuls of the colorful ribbons from one of the drawers and scrubs at his hands with them, scattering them on the floor and reaching for more. He bumps one of the glass vases on the drainboard, and it falls into the sink and shatters. Still clutching bunches of ribbons, he crosses to a door he has not checked. Dropping one handful of ribbons, he opens the door and discovers a powder room, which he enters, snapping on the wall switch beside the door. The fluorescent lights on either side of the mirror blink once, go dark, blink again, flutter and go on.

Look
—now and forever—
at Ronnie Mandeville.

His flesh in the cruel chemical light is gray and lifeless. His left eye, swollen almost shut, is stuffed with blue and brown dead blood. His nose is spread flat upon his face, swollen and red to his cheekbones. One nostril is ringed with caked blood. The cut below his fat vomit-flecked lips has opened and a drop of blood swells there, about to flow down his chin. Dirt from his father's grave has been smeared and wiped with the sweat on his forehead, and there is a large vomit stain on the chest of his jacket. But the eyes; the eyes are the worst. One is almost shut; the other is sunken and red-rimmed, inflamed, blood-shot.

Ronnie stares in fascinated horror at the face. He drops the remaining handful of ribbons on the floor and continues to watch the mirror. After, he raises his hands beside his head with the palms open so he can see them in the glass. They are filled with worms and maggots, slimy, squirming; boring into his flesh. His scream is cut short by Hank's face leering at him from the mirror.

Ronnie's fist, its ribbon fluttering, drives into his father's face, smashing the mirror. He bolts from the room and out the back door and off the porch into the waist-deep snow. But he is mired. With each stride he sinks to mid-thigh as he works his way slowly, frantically across the yard under the shadow of the house toward the front road where his car sits in the buffeting sun-blown wind.

As Ronnie kicks high into the sunlight at the edge of the shadow, he hears the gunfire from the house. He sits down slowly in the deep snow. Three shots, he thinks, although he cannot tell for sure. It seems more comfortable for him to lie than sit, and as he settles back, he looks at the house and sees the rifle sticking through an open second-story window.

It cracks and smokes again.

Relaxed, he touches a hand to his chest—lazily, drowsily—and when he looks at the hand, it is covered with blood. He gently puts the hand in the snow and stares at the cloudless sky. The wind flaps the collar of his jacket against his jaw.

A door slams and he hears people running toward him. He has fallen into the sunlight, just beyond the shadow, and the rising sun warms him.

"It's the Mandeville boy," he hears Stevens, the undertaker, say. The man is standing on the plowed driveway a short distance away. The deep snow blocks Ronnie's view, so that he can see the man only from the waist up. Stevens wears a purple silk bathrobe and heavy black-rimmed eyeglasses. His hair, normally greased smooth, is tousled from sleep. His son, Timothy, trots up beside him. Only a white tee shirt covers his thin chest against the wind. The boy says:

"Did you know it was him?"

"How could I?" Stevens answers. "Look at his face. I couldn't tell." The man shifts his position and Ronnie sees that he is holding a thirty-ought-six deer rifle. Ronnie prefers to look at the cloudless sky.

"Is he dead?" the boy asks his father.

"I don't know. Run in the house and call Dr. Whiting and the police chief. Bring my boots and a jacket when you come back."

The boy trots away and there is silence, except for the erratic wind. Stevens ejects a shell from his rifle.

Ronnie sees Forgione standing at the edge of the snow with the undertaker.

"What happened?" the big fighter asks. He is red-eyed and confused in the morning light.

"I shot him," Stevens says.

Forgione wades through the snow to Ronnie's side. "Shit. He's a mess," he shouts back to Stevens.

"Is he dead?" Stevens asks, leaning over the counter of snow.

"I can't tell," Forgione says. "He's such a mess. Did you call a doctor?"

"Yes," Stevens answers.

The waitress is standing next to the undertaker, her gigantic breasts leaning on the edge of the snow. She begins to sob.

Forgione takes Ronnie's wrist and feels for his pulse.

"Can you get it?" Stevens asks.

"I don't know how to do it," Forgione tells him.

Ronnie hears Timothy Stevens trot up to his father, and he sees the man putting on his jacket and boots. He glances at Forgione's strained face but he prefers looking at the cloudless sky. He can hear Stevens, his son and the waitress wading through the snow toward him.

"Did you get the doctor?" Stevens asks the boy, as he grasps Ronnie's wrist.

"No. He's at the hospital. I didn't know who else to call."

"I don't think we need one anyway," Stevens says, dropping Ronnie's wrist. He is still holding his rifle in one hand. The waitress begins to cry again.

"Clifton said he'd be right over," Timothy Stevens says, referring to the police chief.

They are all silent except for the waitress. Forgione asks:

"Why did you shoot him?"

"I couldn't tell who he was," Stevens answers. "I thought he was a ghoul. I have the departed stored here during the non-burial months. They're in there." He points to the upstairs servants' quarters of the carriage house. They can hear the sirens of the approaching police car.

"He was looking for his father," Forgione tells him.

"I was just protecting my property," Stevens says.

The black police car wheels up the driveway and around the corner of the house, its blue light revolving and its siren dying as it stops next to them.

"I thought he was a ghoul, Clifton," Stevens shouts to the man as he steps from the car and slams the door.

"Is he dead?" the chief asks. He wears his brown uniform and the mirror-front sunglasses. The four people near Ronnie move back to let him through.

"I think so," Stevens says. "I can't get a pulse."

The chief bends over Ronnie and takes his wrist. "He's wearing two different socks," he says.